MYSTERY OF THE
ALL-SEEING EYE

SECRET SUPER SPIES

MYSTERY OF THE ALL-SEEING EYE

MAX MASON

ILLUSTRATED BY
DOUGLAS HOLGATE

Quill Tree Books
An Imprint of HarperCollinsPublishers

alloyentertainment
Produced by Alloy Entertainment
1700 Broadway, New York, NY 10019
www.alloyentertainment.com

ISBN 978-0-06-291569-6

Typography by Joel Tippie
21 22 23 24 25   PC/LSCH   10 9 8 7 6 5 4 3 2 1
❖
First Edition

To all the real-life Maddies out there

MYSTERY OF THE
ALL-SEEING EYE

CHAPTER 1

Condemnant quod non intellegunt.
They condemn what they do not understand.

Maddie Robinson hoped she would win the Eastern Regional Engineering and Robotics Competition. She always did, in some way, but she never won first place. Or second. Or third. She always won a prize the judges seemed to have made up on the spot just for her: the Special Achievement Award. Or the Medal of Impressive Intent. Or the Holy Crud, Congrats on Building Something That Even Looks Like an Invention trophy.

This time, though, Maddie felt like she had a real chance. Her invention—a wireless, two-way charging system, which she called an Electrical Enhancer—was something that had never been done before.

It wasn't perfect; its energy efficiency was low and the device itself looked like a DVD player with the top ripped off, but it laid the groundwork for a brand-new way of powering the world. So she entered the competition anyway.

This invention is truly groundbreaking, she told herself. *I could change the world.*

She was right. She would change the world. But she had no idea how dangerous changing the world would be.

Maddie sprinted inside the Philadelphia Convention Center with her gear nearly spilling out of her arms. It was 9:27, half an hour after the competition officially began. The bus near her house had been delayed, so of course,

she'd missed the transfer to her second bus that she took to the train. Other competitors flew in from private schools in faraway cities to attend, but Maddie lived in Philly—it just so happened that it was the only competition she could get to.

And I can barely even get to this one! Maddie thought. By the time she arrived, her palms (and armpits) were sweaty from worry (and running).

She'd entered the event on her own—her school told her they didn't have it in the budget to sponsor her fifty-dollar entry—so she was stuck on the second floor with the other solo entrants. Mr. Johnson, her science teacher, had looked genuinely apologetic when he gave her the news. But her public school in Franklinville, like its students, didn't have much money. In the end, she and her cousin Jessica baked a hundred cookies and sold them to their friends for fifty cents each to raise money.

As she set up her table, Maddie blew her blond bangs out of her eyes and peeked over the railing to get a look at the fancy-school students below. Everyone else was showing off their work on flashy touch screens or with 3D-printed models.

Maddie sighed. She hadn't even had time to make a trifold poster because she was busy wiring her project together until the very last minute. She knew her invention was what really mattered—she just hoped it would be enough.

Turned out, she'd been worried about being late for

nothing. After waiting for hours, the gaggle of blue-ribbon-wearing judges finally came up to the second floor. Maddie read the judges' name tags. They included top scientists from Ivy League schools, an engineer from Lockheed Martin who Maddie had read about in the *Journal of Micro-electromechanical Systems*, and designers from companies like Google and LyonCorp.

Maddie smiled at the judges, eager to tell them about her invention.

But the judges frowned immediately when they spotted Maddie's booth. "No poster?" asked an old, bearded MIT professor. "No summary paper? Not even a sign? How are we supposed to know what we're looking at?"

After a long morning examining booth after booth of projects, the judges looked sweaty and bored. Maddie got the sinking suspicion they were only walking through the second floor to make the no-chance competitors there feel like they had a shot.

"Oh, well—" Maddie hesitated.

Before she could explain herself, another judge, a woman from Google wearing red lipstick and glasses, jumped in. "Be nice, Dr. Siegel," she said. "The students on the second floor are"—she paused to search for the right, delicate words—"from backgrounds of non-superior opportunity."

Wow, Maddie thought. *Never heard it put like that before.* "Underprivileged." "Disadvantaged." Adults were always coming up with new ways to say "poor."

A judge wearing a Stanford University hoodie, no doubt a tech dude from a fancy company, eyed Maddie's machine skeptically. "So . . . it's a cell phone charger?" he said.

"Yes!" said Maddie. "It's actually—" But before she could start to explain her breakthrough and how her Electrical Enhancer could actually suck power from one device and send it wirelessly to another, the man from Stanford cut her off.

"Seen plenty of those today," he said. "Is there anything that makes this more than *just* a kit you can buy at a hobby store?"

The old judge from MIT scoffed, "You mean besides the fact that without a case on it, it presents a huge risk of electric shock?"

The female judge from Google laughed. The shrill sound hurt Maddie's ears.

The old judge's eyebrows were knitting together like two furry caterpillars. She wanted to shout, *Give me a chance!* but the words stayed stuck in her throat.

"This is a very nice piece of work you've made," the woman from Google said, nodding at Maddie and speaking slowly and softly. "A good effort with the resources you had."

The other judges grunted in agreement and began heading toward the other exhibits.

Maddie knew she had only moments to get the judges' attention before it was too late. With their backs turned to her, she called out, "I built the telemetry system myself!"

All the judges stopped in their tracks.

"To measure the energy flow? You built it . . . yourself?" asked the bearded judge, a look of shock on his face.

"Umm, yes. The off-the-shelf ones have a limited range," Maddie explained. Even though she might not have had all the brand-new parts the others built with, she knew her invention was sound. And she knew the judges would have to listen to her now that she'd started explaining her invention.

The judges' faces went slack, then tightened up, then went all wiggly again as they tried to understand how a twelve-year-old girl on the second floor of a regional engineering competition could design and build a piece of hardware that most adult engineers didn't fully understand.

"I wanted a greater charging distance. So I built my own. In my lab."

"You have a lab?" asked the judge from Lockheed.

Maddie looked down at her shoes. "Well, no," she admitted. "I mean, I don't have a *real* lab. It's just a storage space in the basement of my cousin Jessica's apartment. I live with her." The judges looked at one another and then back at Maddie. She recognized the look on their faces.

"Then let me compliment you again," said the woman from Google, beaming. "This is clearly more than just a nice piece of work. This is a shining example of hard work and personal grit." She looked at her fellow judges. "I think we know who the winner of this year's Bootstrap Award for Determination will be," she said, winking at Maddie. The other judges smiled. One of them threw in a thumbs-up.

Maddie sighed. Another year, another meaningless award. Another group of adults who'd misunderstood her.

"Wow. It would be an honor," was all she could manage to say back.

CHAPTER 2

Alea iacta est.
The die is cast.

Maddie felt dejected. She wanted to pack up and head home right on the spot. But there were a few more hours left before the competition was over, and the rules said you had to stay the entire time.

"Tough break," said the boy at the next booth over. He looked bored sitting next to his model volcano.

Maddie shrugged. "I'm used to it."

"They hated mine, too," said her neighbor. "'Too basic,' they said."

"At least yours looks volcano-y," said Maddie. "Mine looks like it got run over on the way here."

"Yeah," was all the boy said. The way his eyes lingered

on her invention made her sink down farther into the plastic chair behind the display table. She pulled out her book, *A Theoretical Discourse on Electromagnetic Waves.*

"Hmm. A cell phone charger . . . ," a voice said.

Maddie looked up to see a man approaching her table. He was wearing a nondescript gray suit, and he had a sharp nose and a round face. Or maybe he had a bulbous nose and a tiny little face. Or did he have a square jaw and an upturned nose? He was instantly forgettable. It was like the man had been designed in a laboratory by the world's most boring scientists to look as generic as possible. He left no impression at all.

The man looked over Maddie's project.

Yup. And that's all it is, thought Maddie, giving up.

"But that's not all it is," said the man.

Maddie perked up as the man said, "Looks like you've created your own multiwave transference system. Impressive. What does it do?"

"Yes!" Maddie couldn't believe it. "Let's say my cell phone was low on battery," she started explaining. "I could use the machine to take power from your phone and send it over to mine."

"You mean you could steal my phone's power," he said.

Maddie's cheeks got hot. "Well," she said, "I'd say I'm *borrowing* your power, but . . ."

The man chuckled, and Maddie looked at him more closely. He was wearing a ribbon, like the other judges, but instead of a cheap blue rectangle, he had a silken, gold triangle clipped to his shirt. And unlike everyone else at the competition, he wasn't wearing a name tag. "Are you a judge?" Maddie asked. "What company are you from?"

The man looked right into Maddie's eyes, pointedly. "The philosopher Sartre tells us that all people are judges. But Hobbes believed only an extraordinarily wise, all-powerful sovereign is capable of judging." The man continued, "Did the judges here seem to possess true wisdom? Or true power?"

"Not exactly," said Maddie, thinking that was the understatement of the century.

The man picked up Maddie's project and grimaced. "Horrible build quality," he noted. "What does your power loss look like?"

"Around twenty percent."

"Useless," he said, showing no concern for Maddie's feelings at all.

"I could get that down to five percent with silver conduction rods," she added quickly.

"And yet you didn't."

"My school doesn't . . . My cousin only has so much . . ." Maddie didn't like making excuses. Especially this excuse. But she didn't know how else to say it. "I could only afford to use graphite rods," she told him.

For a few seconds that went by as slowly as an ice age, the strange, unmemorable man said nothing. Then he put

Maddie's Electrical Enhancer back on the table. "Let me ask you something. You extended your machine's range so you could steal—"

"Borrow—"

"Power across long distances. You could have turned your prototype's range all the way up and de-powered every other project in the competition. No one here can even figure out what your machine does. They'd never know it was you. Their loss would be your victory. Why didn't you do it?"

The man was still looking right into Maddie's eyes. But she didn't look away. The truth was, she had thought about sabotaging the other projects. Or, at least, she knew it was technically possible.

So what stopped me? she asked herself. But she knew the answer. "I know what it's like to have something taken from you," she said quietly. Maddie's parents—scientists, like her—had disappeared two years ago on a research expedition to the North Pole. She missed them every day. "I didn't want to take anything from anyone else."

No doubt about it, that was an excellent answer. True, heartfelt, and sympathetic. And then the man, the only person in the building, maybe even in the entire city of Philadelphia, who actually understood what Maddie could do . . . rolled his eyes.

"Well, *that's* a surefire way to lose a competition," he said.

"What?" Maddie was shocked.

11

"Still," the man went on, "you have a unique intellect. Your intelligence could make you very powerful, Maddie Robinson."

Maddie gasped. "Wait," she said. "How did you know my name? I never told you."

Who is this mystery man? What does he want?

"You're wearing a name tag," he said.

"Oh . . . right," said Maddie awkwardly. "What's your name?"

"Archibald. Archibald," he said.

"You don't have to say it twice," said Maddie.

"I didn't. My name is Archibald Archibald," he said. "And I never repeat myself. I am the Recruiter."

"A recruiter? For what company?"

"Not a recruiter. THE Recruiter." Archibald extended his fingers toward Maddie. "Here, take my card." It took Maddie a second to see what he was holding: a small, totally see-through business card that looked like plastic or glass. It was practically invisible. Even stranger, there was no information written on it at all. "Go ahead," he said. "It's not radioactive."

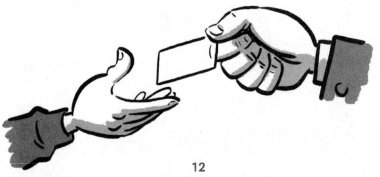

Maddie took the card. It was as flexible as a piece of paper but wouldn't rip or tear or even crease in the slightest. She looked it over from every angle, but it still appeared completely transparent. She held it up to the light—nothing. Then she held it tightly in the darkness of her clasped hands—nothing. She rubbed it in between her palms to see if the heat would make something appear. But nothing happened. She sniffed it, but it didn't smell like anything. She'd been given the fanciest, least helpful business card in the world.

"I'm not sure how you use this thing, but—" Maddie said, and looked up. The man with the oval face and the hawk nose (or was it a slim face and an aquiline nose?) had disappeared.

"Mr. Archibald?" She looked up and down the hallway, but he was gone.

Now all Maddie had was a losing science project, a business card she couldn't read, and an hour-and-forty-five-minute bus ride home.

CHAPTER 3

Ad meliora
Toward better things

It was eight p.m. by the time Maddie made it back to her cousin's apartment building. She had stayed late at the competition to give her address to the frazzled woman in charge of the awards, who promised to mail Maddie a "stupendously glorious" plaque, not that she had any place to hang it up.

Maddie held her sort-of-award-winning Electrical Enhancer under one arm as she unlocked the lobby door and trudged up to the fourth floor. She knew her cousin Jessica was working late, and she guessed Jessica's husband, Jay, was in his usual spot: in the lumpy recliner in the living room, watching baseball on TV.

She'd guessed right.

"Get that, Philly! Catch that!" she heard Jay shouting at the TV as she walked in. "What's good, Maddie? How was school?" he asked.

"It's Saturday, Jay. And it's June. School's ended," Maddie replied, deadpan.

Jay didn't take his eyes off the TV. "Uh-huh," he said. "How do you miss that catch? YOU GOTTA CATCH THAT!" he shouted, as if the players could hear his coaching through the television.

Maddie rolled her eyes and walked through the living room into the small kitchen. She joked—to herself, of course—that it was called the living room because that was where she lived. Jessica and Jay had been kind to take her in after her parents disappeared, but they didn't have a lot of room. It was a one-bedroom apartment, so for the last two years Maddie had been sleeping on their couch, piling her clothes and belongings next to it. She was always trying to stay out of the way. She did her homework at the minuscule coffee table in front of the couch, sitting on the floor. She got dressed in the bathroom, and never kept any personal belongings beyond the bare essentials: only three books, one stuffed animal (an old Snoopy, missing an ear), and a framed photo of her parents, holding her as a baby, taken next to the "Rocky" statue in front of the Philadelphia Museum of Art. Maddie hoped her parents would be proud of her, but she couldn't help feeling alone without them.

15

Two years ago, Maddie's parents had left for a short research trip to study global warming and climate change at the North Pole. But their entire crew had gone missing. Maddie liked to remind herself that they could still technically be alive, even though she knew it was unlikely. Each and every rescue mission had come up empty-handed.

"How come you're never out at the park with the other girls?" Jay asked, for what felt like the hundredth time. "I bet some of them are cool."

"Yeah, they are cool," was all Maddie could say. She didn't mention the rest: that the kids at school all laughed when they saw her in the same three outfits every week, with a hand-me-down backpack and carrying her inventions. Maddie had learned not to mind. Besides, she would rather be inventing, anyway.

She nuked a frozen mushroom pizza and took it downstairs to her basement laboratory. Sure, it was technically the apartment building's laundry room, but Maddie had her own table in the corner and her own shelf to hold all her tools—though she was frequently interrupted by neighbors carrying hampers of dirty clothes.

She liked working next to the gurgling of the washing machines and the whir of the dryers. Yes, there was a dank basement smell down there, but it was overlaid with the meadow freshness and spring lavender scents of detergent and dryer sheets, which Maddie found comforting. Sometimes the click-clack of a zipper or change left in a pocket sounded like a tambourine as she secured wires and soldered electrical components together.

As she sat at her workbench and nibbled her cold-in-the-middle pizza, she took Archibald Archibald's card from her pocket. It still had nothing on it.

"Just a clear piece of . . . something," Maddie mumbled to herself, realizing she couldn't even tell what material the card was made of. "There's got to be more to this. Why else would he give it to me?" It seemed like some sort of test. One that Maddie was determined to ace.

She held the clear card above her head and shouted, "You will not defeat me, business card! YOU WILL REVEAL ALL YOUR SECRETS TO ME!"

Maddie heard a cough behind her. She turned around to see Mrs. Dubrow from the third floor, holding a laundry basket overflowing with her husband Walt's white underwear.

"Oh, I—" Maddie started, her face turning red.

"That's okay. I'll come back, dear," Mrs. Dubrow said, and turned around.

Maddie laid Archibald's nearly invisible business card on her table and got to work.

It must react to something. But what? Maddie wondered as she opened her toolbox. She took out her laser pointer, normally used for making precise measurements, and shined it at the card. Frontward, backward, through a prism, bounced off a mirror. Every which way. But nothing happened.

Maddie dipped the card in water. Nothing.

She rubbed it with negative-109-degree dry ice, which she kept in a special compartment under her worktable. Nothing.

She held it up to the flame of her Bunsen burner. Nothing.

She brushed it with iodine, then hydrogen peroxide, then lemon juice, then every other liquid in her kit. She even ran upstairs and grabbed some ketchup from the fridge and dribbled it on the card, then licked it off. Nothing.

She hooked the card up to jumper cables and a car battery and sent a dozen volts through it. Nothing!

She tried whispering to the card, "Please, please do

something," just in case it was activated by sound waves. Nothing!

She even banged it with a hammer, which she didn't think would do anything, but it felt good.

Nothing made the card react, or even damaged it at all.

Only one thing left to try, thought Maddie. She put on her welder's mask and turned her homemade plasma torch to the highest setting. Just as she was about to burn the card to a crisp, she heard a cough.

Maddie turned around. "Oh, I—" she said, her mask muffling her speech.

It was Mrs. Dubrow again with a slightly terrified look on her face, still holding Walt's underwear.

"I'll come back, dear," she said again, and turned around.

Maddie turned off the torch. She was stumped, which only made her focus even harder. She started walking around the room, which helped her think. "What do I know about the card?" she asked herself.

Only that an extremely odd man gave it to me.

And what did he tell me about it? Nothing. He only said, *Go ahead. It's not radioactive.*

She gasped. "Wait a minute! That's it! Of course! The card isn't radioactive . . . yet!"

CHAPTER 4

Arte et marte
By skill and valor

Jessica and Jay were sprawled on the couch when Maddie burst back into the apartment. Jessica looked tired after a long shift working at the nursing home, wisps of red curls escaping from her braid and dark circles under her eyes. "Maddie, honey, do you need the couch?" she asked, but Maddie was already running to the kitchen.

"No time for sleep!" Maddie said as she unplugged the microwave and lugged the heavy, radiation-emitting appliance through the living room.

Jay didn't take his eyes off the TV. "You break my microwave, you're buying me a new one," he said.

"Oh, let her use it," said Jessica.

"She's the reason we don't have a toaster oven anymore!" Jay groused.

"Did you win your competition?" asked Jessica.

"Not exactly," said Maddie.

"Maddie," said Jessica, "those other kids wish they could do what you do. Even the judges don't understand what you've made half the time!"

"Thanks, Jess," said Maddie. She turned to Jay. "Sorry about the toaster oven. I needed the thermal fuse!" Maddie awkwardly wedged the apartment door open with her foot while trying to balance the heavy microwave in her arms.

"I need a toaster strudel!" Jay said to no one in particular.

Back downstairs, Maddie quickly plugged in the microwave and stuck Archibald Archibald's card in the center. "Let's see what irradiating its molecules does," she said to herself as she set the microwave on high for one minute.

Nothing happened as the seconds ticked down. But then, for one fraction of a second, the card lit up.

There is something on there, Maddie realized. *But I'll need a lot more power to get to it.*

Excitedly, she began taking the microwave apart. She carefully avoided the magnetron, which contained a poisonous metal. Then she removed the microwave's voltage capacitor. Finally, to maximize the microwave's power, she replaced it with her Electrical Enhancer.

Maddie's hand reached for the microwave's power

button, but she put on her welder's mask, just to be safe.

"Okay, here we go!" Before she lost her nerve, she pushed the start button. The microwave began to whir. The lights in the building began to flicker on and off. The card began to glow. "It's working!" she shouted.

The microwave glowed brighter and brighter. As the seconds ticked down, more and more power flowed into the microwave. Lights all around her blinked on and off, extra dim and then extra bright. From the small window, Maddie could see the lights in the building across the street flickering on and off, too. The card started to give off its own light. Car alarms and emergency sirens began to wail.

Maddie heard a loud *POP* of bursting glass as all the streetlights on her block blew up like firecrackers and then . . .

Ding!

The microwave stopped.

"Whew," said Maddie. "That could've been much wor—"

BAM!

The door of the microwave exploded off its hinges and flew right past Maddie's head into the wall behind her.

Standing in the doorway was Mrs. Dubrow again. Her hair was frizzled with static electricity, and she was holding a pair of underwear that had been charred black by the microwave.

"Maybe I won't come back," she said.

"Sorry, Mrs. Dubrow." Maddie quickly grabbed the card

from what was left of the microwave. It was glowing with an illustration of an owl and a motto in Latin:

"Knowledge. Strength. Power," Maddie translated. And below that, two mysterious words that would change everything: *Congratulations, Recruit.*

CHAPTER 5

Carpe diem.
Seize the day.

Maddie quickly unhooked the Electrical Enhancer from the microwave and ran upstairs. The hallways were dark. Maddie looked out the hallway window on her floor. The whole *neighborhood* was dark.

Jessica was lighting candles and placing them around the apartment when Maddie tiptoed inside.

"You just blacked out all of Philly!" Jay said to Maddie. "With *my* microwave!"

"Relax," said Jessica. "It's not like anyone knows Maddie is respons—"

Just then, there was a knock at the door.

Maddie, Jessica, and Jay looked at one another, frozen.

"Maddie?" Jessica whispered.

Someone knows it was me! thought Maddie. *But how? And so quickly! What will I—*

KNOCK.

KNOCK.

Finally, Maddie opened the door and held a candle up.

"Hello, Maddie," said a somewhat familiar-looking man on the other side.

"Hello?" said Maddie.

"Archibald Archibald," he said. "From the competition."

"Oh! I didn't recognize you!" said Maddie.

"Thank you."

Maddie looked at him quizzically. She was sure she was in trouble. "I'm so sorry about the blackout! I didn't mean to! I turned my machine all the way up, like you said, but—"

Archibald cut her off. "Congratulations."

"What?" Maddie didn't understand.

Jessica and Jay looked at each other, even more confused. "Maddie?" asked Jessica. "Do you know this man?"

Archibald stepped into their apartment. "My name is Archibald Archibald. I am the Recruiter. I saw Maddie's invention at the engineering competition earlier today. I'm here to offer her a place in a very exclusive summer camp run by a well-funded international organization. A place where the extraordinary go to train and become extra-extraordinary. Maddie would continue her research in her own laboratory with every resource at her disposal."

He handed Jessica a glossy pamphlet with *Camp Minerva* printed on the front cover. Maddie snagged the pamphlet from her cousin's hands and saw pictures of kids playing in front of cabins and creating inventions in what looked like a *real* science laboratory.

"Really?" Maddie smiled. *Extraordinary?* she thought. Her parents had always teased her, calling her their "little genius." And Jessica always told her that she was creating things "way beyond what most people can understand." And now, finally, there was someone else in the world who recognized what she could do!

"Maddie, that sounds wonderful," Jessica said. Then she sighed. "But I'm sorry, you know we can't afford to send you to camp." She looked at Archibald with a careful eye. "Or off with a stranger."

Before Maddie could object, Archibald spoke. "I am here on behalf of my employer. He wishes to sponsor Maddie's entire stay. Perhaps you have heard of him? Zander Lyon?"

The name hit Maddie's ears like a thousand pounds of glitter and confetti. "Zander Lyon? *The* inventor, explorer, tech genius? That Zander Lyon?" He was Maddie's hero.

"That's the computer dude who's always jumping into volcanoes or whatever?" asked Jay.

Maddie practically screamed.

She'd read everything about Zander Lyon, including his autobiography, *Zander Lyon: Genius at Play*, and his work-out book, *The Zander Zone*, and she'd even subscribed to his weekly newsletter of inspirational musings, *Zanecdotes*. "He built LyonCorp, the company that transformed how a billion people communicate! Now he's building rockets! He'll probably be the first man on Mars!"

She ran to the coffee table and picked up her copy of Zander's autobiography, one of the three books she owned. The billionaire inventor wore a self-assured smile and an overly complicated goatee.

27

"I don't know if I trust this dude," said Jay. "Even his beard looks like it's from the future!"

Archibald Archibald nodded. "Mr. Lyon considers it his job to help create a better future. And he believes Maddie will be an important part of that plan."

"I—I'm—" Maddie couldn't decide whether she should scream or run around the room with joy. She'd spent half of last summer at a garbage dump searching for machine parts and the other half in a musty basement, trying to piece them together by herself.

And now, she thought, *the smartest, coolest, and, oh, did I mention smartest person in the world thinks I could be like him?*

"Jessica, please, please, please can I go? I have to go! Please!" She could tell her cousin wasn't convinced. "Besides, I bet Mom and Dad would have wanted me to go."

Jessica sighed, a bit nervously. "Are you sure, Maddie? You know I love having you here—but I also know it's not the most fun place for a kid."

Maddie looked at her cousin. She looked at Archibald Archibald.

"I'm a hundred million percent sure!" she said. "When do I leave? Next week? Next month?"

Archibald clicked his heels together. "The poet Silius Italicus says, 'Make haste! The tide of Fortune soon ebbs.'"

"Huh . . . ?" Jay looked confused.

"We leave at once. Pack your things, but you won't need

much. You'll get a Camp Minerva uniform and some other supplies. We'll leave as soon as I talk over some small details with your caregiver here and have her sign a few forms."

"Thank you, thank you, thank you!" Maddie grabbed her backpack from under the couch and stuffed some socks, underwear, T-shirts, and her extra pair of jeans into it. She rushed to the bathroom to grab her toothbrush, comb, and bubble-gum-flavored dental floss. Lastly, she grabbed her stuffed animal, Snoopy, from behind a couch cushion.

When she looked up, she saw Jessica signing a stack of official-looking papers, while Jay played a football video game on the TV. Jessica wrapped Maddie into a tight hug, squeezing her so close that Maddie could smell her cousin's signature coconut shampoo. "You're *certain* you want to do this?" she whispered in Maddie's ear.

"Absolutely," said Maddie. "I'll miss you, but I really want to go. I think it'll be good for me. Besides, won't you and Jay like to have your living room free for a little while?" She gave Jessica another squeeze. Jessica tried to pretend she didn't have a tear in her eye and Jay even got up from the TV—the closest he ever got to paying attention to something that wasn't a ball game—and patted Maddie on the shoulder. "We'll miss you, Maddie," he said, surprising both Maddie and Jessica.

"Just remember," said Jessica, holding Maddie close, "you're on a different wavelength from most people, but that's what makes you special. Don't forget that."

Archibald Archibald cleared his throat. Maddie ran to the door.

"Bon voyage!" Jessica called, giving Maddie a kiss on the forehead.

"You owe me a new microwave!" Jay called, his focus back on his game controller.

Outside the apartment building, Archibald Archibald led her to a slightly beat-up-looking pale blue minivan parked on the street. It was covered in peeling bumper stickers: *Give a Hoot for Owls* and *I Brake for Tuba Music*. There was no license plate—just a small golden triangle where one would normally be.

Something about the symbol made her heart beat faster. Where had she seen it before?

Archibald Archibald clicked a key fob, which made an unusual three-note beep, opening the minivan's sliding door. Maddie climbed into the back seat, Archibald taking the seat next to her. The inside of the van was the opposite of the outside: sleek chrome accents, buttery leather seats in pale blue and gray, high-tech panels on the inside walls, and a clear mini-fridge stocked with soda and snacks in the center. The interior was perfectly air-conditioned, and soft music played—sounding somewhat like a cross between a circus and a cartoon soundtrack. Maddie noticed something strange about the front seats: they weren't there.

There was no driver . . . and no steering wheel, either!

The front window was covered in floating info screens, but they were translucent enough that you could still see the road. *I've never seen a car like this,* thought Maddie, *because cars like this don't exist!* The van had been hiding in plain sight, concealing its true nature.

"To Camp Minerva," said Archibald. The car's dashboard lit up and the engine purred. The car turned into the street and took off, driving entirely on its own.

This is the coolest vehicle I've even been in, she thought as the minivan piloted itself down the streets of her Philadelphia neighborhood. She'd heard of self-driving cars but had never seen—let alone ridden in—one like this before.

"Interesting music," Maddie said, trying to make conversation and hide her nerves.

"Thank you," said Archibald Archibald. "It's my demo. I can give you a copy, if you'd like. My day job pays the bills. But my real passion is the tuba."

"Wow," said Maddie. "It sounds, um, very passionate." She held up the Camp Minerva pamphlet. "So, what's the real story with this summer camp?"

"Real story?" asked Archibald, with a shocked look on his face.

"If this were really a camp for exceptional students, I would know about it already. How could you keep a place like this a secret?"

Archibald nodded. "Keeping secrets is of the utmost importance in our organization."

"Organization?" Maddie asked.

Archibald's voice turned serious, and he fixed Maddie with his unnervingly unremarkable gaze. "Maddie," he began, "I have a question for you."

"Yes?" Maddie gulped. There was a long pause. Then he looked even more deeply into Maddie's eyes, as if his next words would be the most important words she had ever heard. Little did she know, they would be.

"Have you ever heard of the Illuminati?"

CHAPTER 6

Secreta revelatum
Secrets revealed

Maddie thought about Archibald's question as the car wove through Philadelphia traffic at top speed. *What's the most polite way to let Archibald Archibald know that he's full-on, banana-pants cuckoo?* she wondered.

"The Illuminati?" she said slowly. "Well, it is a secret society of famous and important people. But it, uh, isn't real. It's just a myth."

"You'll know better soon enough," Archibald Archibald scoffed.

Maddie leaned forward.

Clearly, Archibald Archibald was pulling one over on her. There was no way the Illuminati could be real. No way.

Not possible. Nope, not even a little bit. But as they sat in silence, she couldn't help but secretly wish that Archibald's fantasy was true.

After all, he had given her that fascinating business card. And he knew she'd caused the citywide electrical blackout. And now they were in a car that felt like it was from the future. . . . Maybe there was a chance—even if it was infinitesimally small—that he *was* telling the truth.

After a second, Maddie blurted out, "If the Illuminati are real and you're a part of it, you've got to tell me!"

Archibald kept his face as still as a stone, staring out the window as they passed some brick buildings that were part of the University of Pennsylvania's campus.

"Fine," said Maddie. She took out her phone, a hand-me-down from Jay that only still worked because she'd hacked it. "I'll just cross-reference international databases for the words 'Illuminati,' 'Archibald Archibald,' and 'the Recruiter,' and find out myself."

"Don't bother!" Archibald waved off her idea as though it was a pair of stinky socks. "Anything you find about the Illuminati will be hogwash of the highest order. I'll tell you the *real* story," he said as he straightened out the lapels of his suit.

"The Illuminati were created millennia ago, to bring light to a world of darkness," he explained. "We spread knowledge and peace—and we stop those who spread ignorance, death, and destruction. Our super secret super spies keep the world safe, doing what governments are unable to do. All while hiding in plain sight."

He's got to be joking, right? thought Maddie. "No offense, Mr. Archibald. But a secret society with super spies doing super secret things all over the world? It's impossible."

"Trust me, Recruit. You have no idea what's possible."

Their car made a quick turn down an empty alleyway. A small, cloud-shaped light fixture in the car's ceiling started flashing blue and purple above Maddie. "Is that a 'fasten seat belt' sign?" she asked. "Like on an airpla—?" But before she could finish her sentence, the car suddenly lifted off the ground with a gentle lurch.

In seconds, the car had levitated a dozen feet in the air and angled slightly upward, flying faster and faster across the sky over Center City Philadelphia. Maddie's stomach felt queasy for a few seconds, until she got used to the upward motion. She put her nose to the car's window, peering down at the tops of cars and buildings, as the Philadelphia skyline appeared smaller and smaller. "We're flying!" she yelled. "But won't everyone see us? We're in a flying car! We'll be the top story on tomorrow's news!"

As usual, Archibald's forgettable face showed no expression at all. Maddie leaned over to catch the car's reflection in a skyscraper's windows, but there was nothing there. "Wait. Are we . . . We're invisible?" she shouted, half asking, half overcome with delight. "But how?" Archibald opened his mouth to explain, but Maddie answered her own question. "The car must be bending the light around it!"

Archibald pointed to Maddie's safety belt. "You'll want to put that on."

"Oh, okay—" As Maddie snapped her belt together—*WHIPCRACK!*—the car blasted through the sound barrier.

"Amazing!" Now they soared above the clouds. Maddie craned her neck, enjoying the view of the evening sky, darker than she'd ever seen it in Philadelphia, thanks to the blackout she'd caused. "So aside from building a hypersonic flying car that's also invisible, what else have the Illuminati done?" she asked.

"How's your history?" asked Archibald.

"I'm really more of a math person," Maddie admitted.

"That's fine. Most of what you read in history books isn't true anyway. Or at least not the whole truth. The Illuminati have had a hand in almost every major world event: the signing of the Magna Carta, the writing of the United States Constitution, and humanity's first trips to outer space. We've created inventions that have changed the course of history: the printing press, the cell phone, the electric guitar, and instant cappuccino machines, to name a few. We've also built some quite grand meeting places all over the globe."

Maddie gasped. "Oh my goodness, the Illuminati built the pyramids, didn't they?"

Archibald nodded. "Yes."

"And Stonehenge?"

"Yes."

"And the Leaning Tower of Pisa?"

"Absolutely not!" Archibald looked offended. "If the Illuminati built a tower, it would stand up straight, that I assure you."

"But why all the secrecy?" asked Maddie. "Why not let the whole world know about what you're doing?"

Archibald's face grew more serious, which Maddie had thought wasn't possible. "Have you ever heard of the Great Brooklyn Earthquake of 2014?" he asked.

Maddie searched her memory. "No."

"What about the outbreak of genetically enhanced locusts that struck Wyoming last year?"

"No," said Maddie.

"That's because we stopped those events from happening." Archibald leaned in closer to Maddie. "If the world knew about everything we do, there would be panic. War." Maddie nodded. Archibald continued, "Now you see why we must work in the shadows. And just how important our great work is."

The car began to descend. Maddie's stomach lurched a tiny bit.

"But why me?" she asked. "What does the Illuminati want *me* for?"

Archibald looked out the window as the car touched down. "That question will be answered for you shortly," he said.

The minivan's door slid open and a warm, salty breeze brushed Maddie's face as she stepped out into brilliant sunlight.

She gasped. "Whoa," she said, looking around. She was standing on the white sand of a tropical island, under a banner strung between two palm trees that read *Welcome, Illuminati Recruits.*

Maddie knew her parents had expected big things from her. *But this is* really *big,* Maddie thought. Young people wearing clothes from all over the world were stepping out of minivans all around her with wide eyes, just as amazed as Maddie. Could it be that all the Illuminati's recruits were children?

The sun's heat and the ocean's breeze wrapped around Maddie like a hug from a long-lost grandmother. They had traveled halfway around the globe in mere minutes in an invisible flying car. It seemed impossible. She blinked. She looked up at the beaming sun, through the pointy leaves of a palm tree.

She looked back at Archibald Archibald. "Okay," she said. "Now I believe you."

CHAPTER 7

Credo quia absurdum.
I believe because it is absurd.

Just down the beach, Maddie spotted a centuries-old statue, a marble figure of an explorer. In her hand was a lit golden torch. The inscription on the statue's base read *Camp Minerva*.

Maddie's brain was in overdrive: the biggest myth in the world, the Illuminati, was real.

"Welcome, *willkommen, hwangyong hamnida, kuwakaribisha,* and *bienvenidos,*" said a man wearing an official-looking jumpsuit. "Please head to the camp amphitheater for the Opening Convocation."

Maddie took in her surroundings as she and the other recruits walked on a path of crushed seashells through the

CAMP
MINERVA

campus. It truly looked like a summer camp at first. There were wooden cabins, soccer and baseball fields, and even a swimming hole, surrounded by bushes speckled with colorful tropical flowers. But as she continued down the path, she noticed that beyond the cabins, the island was also dotted with fantastic buildings from every time period in history: stone buildings with imposing marble Roman columns, an orange-and-gold Japanese-style shrine, a Taj Mahal–like library, hanging gardens, something that like looked like an old French cathedral, and even two types of pyramids—one with smooth edges, the other with zigzag, stepped edges.

As Maddie approached the center of the island, one central building dominated the landscape. Overlooking the camp stood an ultramodern skyscraper made of glass and swooping metal and topped by a giant globe, made of some sort of golden metal. Maddie watched as the rooftop globe opened wide and the fleet of flying minivans descended swiftly inside it.

In the shadow of the tower was a small outdoor stage. There were about a hundred other recruits filing into the seating area, some around Maddie's age, most a little older, in all types of clothing, from royal uniforms to hoodies like Maddie's and everything in between. But everyone wore the same expression—excited, a little dazed, and maybe even a bit scared.

Maddie spotted an empty seat on one of the long

benches, next to a boy who looked just as shocked as she was. His unruly curly hair fell over his glasses, and he wore a tweed jacket that was at least two sizes too big. He was as skinny as a blade of grass and a few inches shorter than Maddie, with brown skin and inviting hazel eyes. "Anyone sitting here?" Maddie asked.

"Not yet!" he said, gesturing for Maddie to sit. "I'm Caleb."

"Maddie."

Caleb smiled. "I—"

"Attention, Recruits!" a voice boomed from a hidden loudspeaker, interrupting Caleb. "Welcome to Camp Minerva. Please give your full attention to the head of training, the illustrious Grand Sentinel Yulia Volkov."

A striking woman with high cheekbones and a serious expression marched onto the stage and the crowd fell silent. She wore a light brown military uniform adorned with a patch of a wolf. As Volkov looked over the crowd, Maddie saw that there was a glittering, jewel-like implant where Volkov's left eye should have been. Something about the gleam in it made Maddie's arm hairs stand up on end.

"Whoa," Caleb whispered.

"Hello, Recruits. The fact that you are here means that you know the truth of the Illuminati. But you may wonder why *you* are here." Volkov paused. She had a heavy Eastern European accent and spoke crisply, making each word count. "Since the founding of the Illuminati, we have recruited young people to become the next generation of Illuminati agents. You are quick to learn new skills, to adapt to unexpected challenges. Adults are hard to teach. But you, each and every one of you, can be molded into the world's finest agents: super spies, peacekeepers, disaster averters, historymakers, defenders of the helpless, tireless warriors for knowledge and the advancement of humanity."

Volkov stood as still as a statue while she spoke, but she commanded so much respect that no one could look away. "You are here because someone believes you are exceptional. You are not," she continued coldly.

The crowd started mumbling. Maddie looked at her new friend and they both shrugged.

"Yet! Under my training, you will be. You will work with the best so that you will *become* the best. You will train in your field. And you will learn many new skills as well. Brilliant scientists, decorated generals, and Olympic athletes will be among your teachers this summer."

Maddie's knee started to bounce. The crowd felt electric. Volkov stamped her boot to silence the excitement. A hush fell over the crowd.

She flicked her wrist and a holographic display appeared over the stage. Human-sized 3D renderings of ancient warriors, scientists, and explorers flew to the center of the stage. They looked completely real, even though Maddie knew they weren't. She was itching to find out how they programmed such advanced holograms.

The figures morphed into a massive golden pyramid with a strange eye floating above it. Maddie recognized the image instantly—it was on the back of the dollar bill.

"This is the sigil of the Illuminati," said Volkov. "We each are like the bricks of the pyramid—strong on our own, but together, unbreakable. And the All-Seeing Eye reminds us that the Illuminati watch over the entire world. We work in the shadows to protect humanity. Many well-known individuals have been in our ranks."

Now the holograms shifted, morphing again and again into life-sized figures of dozens of famous Illuminati members. They went by so quickly Maddie could barely make them out, but she was certain she spotted George Washington, Harriet Tubman, Marie Curie, Gandhi, Picasso, and, with immense elation, Zander Lyon. No one could contain their excitement any longer. The whole crowd was on their feet, cheering.

"This is amazing!" Caleb yelled.

Maddie grinned. *Could I really be like those people?* she wondered. *Talented? Brave? . . . Special?*

"Silence!" shouted Volkov. The recruits shrank back down into their seats. "Being a member of the Illuminati is a great responsibility." Volkov turned off the holographic display.

"The work we do is dangerous. Sometimes even deadly. It is possible that the safety of the entire world may one day rest entirely on your shoulders." Maddie looked around. Caleb and several other recruits looked nervous. Volkov was clearly not a woman to mess with. But her firm attitude only made Maddie more determined.

"If you cannot accept such responsibility, you may leave." Volkov gestured to a car stationed on the docks. "On the ride home, you will be given a special serum, and the memory of today will be erased. You will believe it to be only a strange dream. You will go back to your ordinary lives. Please take a moment to decide if this dangerous path is a road you are able to take. If you really have what it takes to be a super secret super spy."

Caleb turned to Maddie. "Are you staying?"

"Yeah, are you?" Caleb looked nervous but nodded yes.

Maddie watched in silence as she counted three or four recruits who got up and left.

Volkov continued, "If you stay, you will no longer be ordinary. You will be undercover agents. Your old lives will be mere cover stories. You will be on call, traveling wherever the world needs you, for an organization that officially does not exist. Keeping a secret such as this will be difficult. But keep it you must."

Maddie wondered if she was ready to give up her old life forever. But as she thought about her life—late nights doing homework on Jessica and Jay's couch, endless bus rides to and from school, eating turkey sandwiches alone at lunch—she realized there wasn't much she would miss.

Sometimes she hung out with her neighbor RayQuan after school, but they mainly just talked about their science homework. She didn't have any true friends.

The Illuminati were offering her a chance to learn, to have adventures, and, maybe, to even change the world. Even with scary Volkov around, it would be worth it.

Maddie smiled widely as she heard Volkov's parting words: "The light will always show the way. Welcome to the Illuminati."

CHAPTER 8

Tabula rasa
A blank slate

Maddie turned to Caleb. His jaw was practically on the ground. "I can barely believe it," he said, still staring straight ahead.

"I can't believe it, either," said Maddie. "But I'd like to."

Caleb gulped. "Me too."

Volkov turned to the recruits one final time as she walked offstage. "And now, a welcome message from the High Consecrator, Keeper of the Wisdom Eternal, and Leader of the Illuminati."

Maddie's phone buzzed in her pocket. Every other recruit must've felt the same buzzing because everyone took out their phones. On each screen was an incoming video call.

"Can everyone see me?" said the voice on the other side. The screens showed the inside of a luxury airliner. "I just wanted to say a quick hello to all you new recruits." He flipped the camera around toward his face. "The name's Zander Lyon."

Maddie gasped. "No way," she whispered to herself. A boy in the row in front of her fainted.

Zander Lyon, the tech billionaire, occasional astronaut, full-time genius, and leader of the Illuminati was talking to her!

"Let me tell you why I invited you here: to change the world. Adults get stuck in their ways! They can't see the future. That's why we need you. Your work is"—he made an explosion gesture—"spectacular. Some of the inventions you've already created are mind-blowing. I was especially impressed by Maddie Robinson's Electrical Enhancer. Is she there?"

Maddie's heart either stopped completely or skipped so many beats that she couldn't tell the difference. *Zander Lyon knows me? Did he just say I was spectacular? Should I say something? Can he even hear me?*

"Yes, hello, Maddie is me," she blurted awkwardly. She waved into her phone. *So much for making a good first impression,* she thought.

"A pleasure to make your virtual acquaintance, Maddie," said Zander. Maddie could feel the eyes of every recruit staring at her. "Sorry I can't be there in person, but you know how it is—work, work, work," he said as he pulled on his skydiving goggles and opened the door on his plane. "Today I'm testing out my Emergency Responder boots. These are the Mark II Personal Thruster prototypes." He clamped two round discs to his leather boots. "Aka Rocket Boots."

Recruits all around Maddie were oohing and aahing at Zander's latest breakthrough. *That's not just next-gen tech,* Maddie thought. *That's omega-generation technology. The future!*

"I won't bore you with the details," said Zander. "They're really more like fusion propellers than rockets—but 'Rocket Boots' has a little more swagger to it, don't you think? I built them to control descent when I'm doing high-altitude skydives. I'd hate to smash into an airplane or one of those—what do you call 'em?—huge, pointy things that stick out of the ground?"

No one dared speak. Except for Caleb. "Mountains?" he guessed.

"Mountains! Yes! Smacking into one of those would be a total buzzkill!" said Zander. He walked to the edge of his plane's open door. "Good luck in your training. Now wish me luck!" Before anyone could say anything, he continued, "Just kidding! I make my own luck." Then he tossed his phone aside and leaped out of his aircraft headfirst.

Maddie's head was buzzing. *Zander Lyon, THE Zander Lyon, thinks my work is mind-blowing?*—when an announcement came over the loudspeakers. "All recruits to the Chow Hall for lunch."

Lunch? Maddie's stomach rumbled with hunger—what time was it back in Philadelphia? This was turning out to be the longest, most exciting day ever.

The Chow Hall was a squat wooden building that appeared long overdue for a fresh coat of paint. And as Maddie got closer, she scrunched up her nose at the greenish tint of mildew on the outer corners of the building. This place needed a renovation.

But suddenly, the rusty screen doors whisked open automatically, and Maddie and the other recruits streamed into a surprisingly bright room—the entire ceiling was made of glass, crisscrossed with large wooden beams. The floor was a honey-colored wood inlaid in a zigzag pattern, and several picnic tables filled the room. Each table had a unique centerpiece. Maddie spotted a cactus, a Venus flytrap, and branches dotted with fluffy pink blossoms. Elegant white napkins were folded into complex origami-like shapes at each place setting.

A short, one-wheeled robot shaped like an exclamation point zoomed up to Maddie. Its black-and-white paint job made it look like it was wearing a tuxedo. "Beep boop," it said robotically. It was carrying a tray of glasses filled with sparkling grape juice. "Ooh, I'd love to see what makes you tick," she said, tapping the robot's side. The bot

beep-beeped nervously, and after Maddie took a glass, it squealed away.

Maddie was struck by the smells: sizzling hamburgers, veggie-covered pizzas, grilled Mediterranean seafood, and even syrup-drizzled pancakes. She could smell cumin and curry, freshly baked brownies, toasting marshmallows, and the mouthwatering scent of barbecued chicken.

Every seat had a different meal in front of it. *There's no way,* thought Maddie, until she spotted it at a back table: a Philly cheesesteak with provolone cheese and sauce dripping off the sides of a seeded hoagie roll, in the distinctive wrapper of her favorite diner in Center City. There was a place card with her name at the top of the plate that read *Recruit Maddie Robinson.* A huge smile spread over her face. As she saw the delighted looks on the other campers' faces, she realized that every camper had been served their absolute most favorite meal in the world.

"Hiya! Looks like we're table buddies!" said a chipper voice. Maddie looked up. Somehow, that cheery voice belonged to a girl who was a full foot taller than Maddie, with half her head shaved and the remaining hair dyed bright blue. She was in overalls, making it hard to miss her suntanned skin and softball-sized arm muscles.

"I'm Lexi! Boy, this place sure is fancy. I sneezed and a little robot handed me a handkerchief!"

Maddie giggled as she sat down. She liked Lexi immediately. "Well, I'm Maddie. Now I've met two people here. Well, three if you count a robot."

"Ha!" Lexi snort-laughed. "How did you get invited? Let me guess—you're, like, a super-genius or something."

"Not really," said Maddie, blushing. "I make stuff. Like, machines. And I do math, too. What about you?"

"Ice-skating, my darling," Lexi said, jokingly waving her arm like a princess. "But that got boring," she added. She flexed her arm muscles. "Now, judo! And some kickboxing and wrestling and whatever else I can learn."

"I'll make sure to be extra nice to you, then," said a boy who took their table's next seat.

"Caleb!" said Maddie excitedly.

"Don't worry, new buddy!" said Lexi. "I kick butt—but only if the butt belongs to a bad guy! I'm Lexi."

"Nice to meet you."

"So what amazing talent do you have?" Maddie asked Caleb.

"Isn't it obvious?" Caleb said as he adjusted his glasses. "I'm a grizzled ice fisherman who once wrestled a five-hundred-pound bluefin—*underwater*—for five minutes."

The girls blinked as Caleb grinned playfully.

"Just kidding. I solve puzzles."

Maddie giggled.

"Like jigsaw puzzles?" asked Lexi.

"Hmm, not exactly," Caleb said. "More like mysteries. For instance, I would guess that Maddie is from a big city, probably Philadelphia. And, Lexi, I'll guess that you're from a farm in Georgia that grows . . . cucumbers."

Maddie looked over at Lexi, whose jaw was dropped wide open. "No. Way. Maddie, did he get you, too?"

"How did you . . . ?" Maddie asked.

Caleb pointed to their plates. "Your favorite foods. Maddie, your sandwich is from a diner or bodega, so it had to be from a big city. And cheesesteak on hoagie rolls is a Philadelphia specialty."

Maddie nodded, impressed.

"And, Lexi," said Caleb, "I guessed a cucumber farm because, well—I've just never seen that many cucumbers on a plate before." Maddie snuck a glance down at the table— Lexi's plate was covered in nothing but sliced, whole, and pickled cucumbers. Mini ones, big ones, regular-sized ones. She and Lexi and Caleb all burst out laughing.

Caleb continued, "Also, Lexi, you have a small spot of dirt on the bottom of your left pant leg. It's reddish-brown. Looks to me like the Cecil soil type, which is slightly acidic, making it one of the rare soils that's perfect for cucumbers."

"Whoa! I never met anyone else who cared about soil types before," said Lexi.

"And what does your food tell us about you?" asked Maddie.

Caleb took a sniff of the tuna and onion sandwich in front of him. "That after lunch, I'll need the universe's largest breath mint."

CRASH!

Maddie turned. At a table behind them, a boy had bumped into another recruit who'd been carrying his plate, sending it flying.

"Pay attention to your surroundings, you klutz!" yelled the recruit who'd dropped his plate. He wore a black turtleneck and black trousers, set off by a silver belt buckle that looked more expensive than all of Maddie's clothes put together. He spoke with a posh English accent. "You owe me a tuna tartare! I was trying to change tables, to find some suitable recruits to dine with."

The other recruit dropped to his knees to help clean up. "Sorry about that! So sorry!" he said in a French accent. "Oh, I'm causing such a mess!" He started to wipe fish chunks off the boy's shoes.

"Don't touch those! You'll probably just ruin them more." By now, the entire Chow Hall was watching the scene.

The French recruit stood up and began speaking just like a Wild West cowboy. "Now wait just a durn minute there, cowpoke. I said I was sorry." Then, just as quickly, he started speaking in a posh British accent, just like the Queen of England! "Forgive me, good lad. I'll send some footmen to fetch you a new pair forthwith!"

The boy with a thousand voices extended his hand and spoke again with a French accent. "Roland Dargil. From Paris, but I've lived all over. Friends call me Rolly. I really am sorry! I knew I was clumsy, but I thought I could go at least one day without screwing something up!"

"Evidently you can't," spat the recruit with the soiled shoes. "The name's Killian Horne. Don't forget it," he finished, not accepting Rolly's handshake. He ran a hand through his blond pompadour instead, which popped against his pale skin. His hairdo flattened momentarily, then sprang back up into the perfectly swooping pompadour again.

Maddie made eye contact with Rolly. "You can do voices! That's really cool," she said, trying to make Rolly feel better.

Killian turned. "Ah. So you're the girl who Zander Lyon was so impressed with." Maddie's shoulders shrank at the attention. "I'm an engineer myself," he said. The way Killian's eyes lingered on Maddie made her feel very small. She knew that look—she'd seen it many times before. It was the expression people gave her when they thought they were better than her.

Killian walked away, leaving Maddie's area in peace.

"Want to sit with us?" she asked Rolly. "I'm sure we can make room."

"Would love to!" Rolly sat down on the bench as Maddie

scooted closer to the other boy at their table. He had short black hair, olive skin, and a crooked tooth that hid behind a shy smile.

The boy pulled up the voice memo app on his phone and said quietly, "Note on Recruit Killian Horne: Egotistical. Vain. Not a prime candidate for friendship."

The dark-haired, olive-skinned boy looked up, realizing that the others could hear him. "My bad," he said nervously. "I'm not used to talking to other people. Did you know you can be the number one player in the world in *Alien Tactics* without ever using voice chat?"

Maddie laughed. "Yeah, that's how I play, too," she admitted. "I'm Maddie, from Philly, and this is Lexi and Caleb."

"I'm Sefu. From Cairo," he replied. He slouched so low in his seat, you could barely see his eyes above the table.

Lexi pointed toward Killian's new table. "By the way, guys, *that's* the type of butt I'd like to kick."

Caleb nodded. "You don't need genius-level observation skills to know that Killian Horne is as slimy as a bathtub full of earthworms."

Maddie looked at Lexi, Caleb, Sefu, and Rolly. She'd already talked to more people at Camp Minerva than she'd talked to at her own school. At home, liking science made her a weirdo. But here, everyone was weird in some way. They were awesome, too. Weirdly awesome.

She smiled at Sefu, remembering his note-to-self about

Killian. "What do you say? Are we prime candidates for friendship?"

Sefu gave a shy smile. "The data points so far indicate yes."

The five recruits clinked their glasses together and laughed. Then everyone dug into their favorite meals.

CHAPTER 9

Fac fortia et patere.
Do brave deeds and endure.

After they'd finished eating, a pack of waiter-bots scurried around to clean up. Volkov appeared in the Chow Hall's doorway. "Free time is over," she said. "Your training begins now."

"Should I ask Volkov if we have time for dessert?" Caleb whispered to his tablemates. "She seems like she could use an ice cream cone."

Maddie started giggling.

"Something funny about training, Ms. Robinson?"

"No! Of course not, ma'am," said Maddie, her voice nearly cracking from nerves. She caught a cold glare from Volkov's bejeweled eye. It felt like a bee sting to the brain.

Maddie wondered what kind of technology was inside it.

"It is time for your first test to determine if you belong here," said Volkov, looking straight at Maddie. "Come. All of you."

Well, she hates me already, was all Maddie could think.

Outside, under a circle of palm trees, Volkov organized the students into groups of six. Fortunately, Maddie's lunch buddies were standing next to her and got put in her group. *Un*fortunately, Killian was nearby and got put in her group, too.

"These are your training units," Volkov announced. "You will spend your summer together. Unless you drop out first."

Maddie was pumped to be in a group with her new friends. She was much less pumped to be working with Killian, who she could already imagine making life harder for her.

Volkov approached their training unit. "Follow me."

She led them toward the giant tower with the globe at the top overlooking the camp. "This is the Obelisk," said Volkov.

"Looks familiar, somehow," said Lexi.

"It's the same shape as the Washington Monument, aside from the globe," said Maddie. "I wonder if it's just a coincidence."

Caleb pointed to the corners of the Obelisk's base. "I don't think the Washington Monument has metal crab feet sticking out of it."

Maddie squinted. There were decorative crab pincers reaching out from underneath the building. "Are these inscribed with Egyptian hieroglyphics?"

Volkov shepherded them into an elevator inside the Obelisk. "This is the most secure building on the planet," she said as the elevator plunged downward. The recruits all grabbed at the elevator walls, trying to gain some sort of balance as they swiftly descended. "It is the Illuminati's headquarters of worldwide operations."

When the elevator doors whooshed open, Maddie was dazzled by rows and rows of gleaming glass-walled chambers and a softly glowing floor. Each chamber was filled with adults in white lab coats or fashionable suits and dresses bustling back and forth, punching buttons on sleek computers sprouting tubes and wires. Clocks set to the times of major world cities lined the outer walls, and floating screens showed live video from all over the planet (plus a few screens that looked to be observing another planet entirely).

They walked down the softly illuminated hallway, then turned a corner and found themselves in a bright atrium lined with columns. Volkov's boots echoed loudly on the marble floor. Statues and busts of historical figures in stone, wood, and bronze filled the room. "The Hall of Inspiration," Volkov announced, "filled with likenesses of Illuminati members of note." As the group passed each work of art, Maddie noticed a statue of Harriet Tubman shifting slightly. Abraham Lincoln adjusted his top hat. As Maddie looked up in awe at the statue of Ada Lovelace, who invented the computer algorithm, the statue head turned to her and smiled. It was incredible.

Maddie thought back to the "Rocky" statue she'd visited with her parents—right outside the Philadelphia Museum of Art. It suddenly seemed a lot less cool than a statue of Gandhi that could look you right in the eyes and nod peacefully at you. She wished more than anything that she could share this moment with her mom and dad.

"How did you get a solid material to do *that*?" Maddie asked with breathless wonder.

Volkov raised her eyebrows. She didn't look impressed. "A simple mix of technology, artistry, and *ingenio maximus*—maximum ingenuity."

Volkov led them forward through a set of automatic doors into a sleek, modern-looking room. "This is our Class IV Technical and Theoretical Scientific Experimentation Laboratory."

Maddie's eyes were drawn to an unkempt corner of the lab. Not only were there loose circuit boards and half-finished gadgets strewn over the tables, but someone had taped a handmade sign to the wall: *Gadget Playground*. "That is where our leader, Zander Lyon, spends most of his time when he is at the Obelisk." Maddie was already itching to make a beeline there when Volkov added,

"Maddie, Killian, as inventors you may familiarize your-self with the facility while I show your fellow recruits other areas of interest." Volkov led the rest of the group out.

Maddie didn't need to be told twice.

As she explored the lab, she was overjoyed. The entire floor was made up of dozens of individual glass-walled experimentation rooms. Maddie sprinted between a room of scientists testing an invisibility spray on each other and a room-sized aquarium where two octopuses appeared to be playing chess. She caught glimpses of researchers testing heat rays, freeze rays, and according to a sign on the wall, something called an "explosion ray."

She headed back to the gadget tables. Bins that lined the walls held every material and component she'd ever wanted to create with. She grabbed handfuls of miniaturized tech, settled herself at an ergonomic workstation, and immedi-ately began taking apart her phone, eager to modify it to superpowered levels. "Let's see," Maddie said to herself, "I'll want to add a sound-wave modifier, an enhanced cam-era lens with 4D capability, a mini holographic projector, an anti-interference shield, and an unbreakable polymer case. Ooh, and upgrading the flashlight to ultrahigh fre-quency? Yes, please!"

She began adding new tech to her phone with surgical precision. Out of the corner of her eye, Maddie noticed Killian reading a message on his smartwatch and then

quickly leaving the lab. She rolled her eyes. "Slacker," she mumbled to an empty room.

Carefully, Maddie fused her phone back together. Her modifications were all hidden inside, and the phone looked indistinguishable from when Jay had first given it to her. As soon as the phone finished powering on, it beeped with a message: Meet on Floor 13. Now.—Volkov

The text was from ten minutes ago! Her stomach dropped as she realized she'd be late to her very first meeting.

Maddie grabbed her phone and quickly stuffed some gear into an Illuminati-branded messenger bag she found hanging on the lab wall. She was mega-annoyed that Killian hadn't even bothered to mention anything to her, and she hightailed it to the thirteenth floor.

There, she spotted Volkov waiting impatiently in the hallway with the other members of Maddie's training group. "Your lack of punctuality has been noted," Volkov said, her jeweled eye glinting with irritation. Maddie's cheeks flushed red.

A door slid open and Volkov led them inside a long, narrow room. "Your first task is to simply get to the other side of the room," said Volkov, pointing to a long ledge just over fifteen feet away. "Remember, this is your team. You may work together . . . or against each other."

Maddie eyed Killian.

"The path to success is yours to discover," said Volkov. On the far side of the room there was a door that said *Exit* in red letters. Volkov walked toward it and then turned around. "Good luck."

"Good luck?" asked Lexi.

Suddenly, Volkov became transparent and began to fade away.

"A hologram!" said Caleb. "But why wouldn't she be here for real?"

"She's probably sick of looking at your face," said Killian. "I know I am."

"Hey!" shouted Maddie. But before she could defend her friend, panels on the walls shifted, revealing dozens of small nozzles.

"What the—?" Caleb and Sefu said at the same time.

And then suddenly the whole room was filled with blazing-hot flames.

CHAPTER 10

Disco inferno.
I learn through suffering.

Waves of heat surged over them. The pillars of flame shot
out from odd angles, creating flameless spaces where a person could step and leap through. But the nozzles rotated in
unpredictable directions—there was no way through without dodging the wild streaks of fire.

Maddie backed up against the door they'd entered
through, beads of sweat forming on her forehead.

"What are we going to do?" Lexi shouted.

"I don't know!" Maddie replied. She couldn't tell if she
was sweating from the heat or from sheer terror.

"Wait . . ." Caleb started analyzing the room. "Ten feet
high, about six and a half feet wide," he said. "That's as
big as a wild male yak."

"What? How is that going to help us?" Maddie asked.

"Is there any chance," asked Lexi, "that one of us is a world-record-holding junior firefighter or something?" The silence spoke for itself. "Anyone bring anything helpful?"

"Just my phone," Maddie mumbled.

The heat in the room grew more intense.

"I was practicing in the dojo," said Lexi. "I've got my portable speaker if we need any motivational pump-up jams."

"I was in the library," said Caleb. "There's some really arcane stuff in there. With my left eye, I was reading *A Brief History of Time* by the theoretical cosmologist Dr. Stephen Hawking—"

"Oh, shut your gob!" yelled Killian. "Are you just trying to annoy me?"

"Me? Annoy you? I would *never*," Caleb said mischievously, trying to annoy Killian even more.

Sefu stepped forward. "Could you two cut it out before we're all burned to a crisp?"

Killian tugged on a lab coat he'd borrowed from the lab. "Enough wasting time. My jacket is fireproof." Killian walked toward the flames, then ran through at full speed. His jacket gave off a bit of smoke, but he was otherwise unharmed. "Good luck, dingbats," he said as he stood safely on the other side of the room.

"If his coat was made of yak fur," said Caleb, "it wouldn't

be fireproof. But it would be highly resistant to static electricity."

Sefu tiptoed toward the flames. Instead of running through them, he was walking as slowly as possible. "I once completed a fire-room puzzle in a first-person video game. It took one hundred eighty-six attempts," he said. "I now know, the secret is patience." He continued forward at a glacial pace. The flames nearly got close enough to flick his nose, but none touched him as he made his journey.

Maddie observed the situation, frozen. There had to be some way out, but she had no idea what it could be.

"How is this so easy for some people?" she said aloud, getting more and more worried about her own escape plan.

Sefu finished his snail-like trek. Free of the flames, he jumped to the far wall and out of harm's way.

Suddenly, the fire-spitting nozzles stopped. Maddie, Caleb, Rolly, and Lexi were still left. Caleb leaned forward. "Maybe we passed by *not* walking through," he said as the nozzles roared back to life. "Or not."

The rotating nozzles of flame were now moving toward them. They would have to find a way through. Or die trying.

"Hurry!" warned Sefu.

"Are you guys scared?" asked Lexi. "Because I'm scared." Maddie and Caleb nodded. "Caleb," Lexi continued, "you're pretty small. I could carry you—"

"NO!" said Caleb. He took a breath. "Sorry. I don't like it when people pick me up."

"I'll take a ride!" Rolly said, eagerly hopping on Lexi's back.

Lexi and Rolly then barreled toward the fire. She hurdled over a row of low flames, then kicked off the wall to reach the far side of the room. Rolly held on for dear life. "Come on, guys," she said. "You can do it!"

Caleb took a step forward. The flames were still moving toward them. "There's got to be a pattern," he said. "It's just a matter of . . . aaaand, I found it." With the flames' seemingly unpredictable pattern in his head, Caleb easily stepped through the labyrinth of fire, spinning, ducking, and dodging at just the right moments. On the other side, he gave a tiny, theatrical bow—and accidentally waved his hand through the final jet of flame. "Ow!" he said. "Anybody pack any ointment?"

Maddie was the only one left on this side of the flames. She was backed up against the door they'd come in through. In less than a minute, the flames would reach her. She fished around in her bag, feeling desperately for anything that might help, when she remembered the sound-wave modifier she'd just added to her phone. "Lexi!" Maddie shouted. "Can you toss me your speaker?"

"Sure!" Lexi tossed the handheld speaker through the flames like a football. Maddie caught it and crouched, took out her tools, and began furiously taking apart her phone and Lexi's speaker.

"Maddie, if you're looking for some music as you turn into

toast," taunted Killian, "I suggest Bartók's Piano Concerto Number Two. It's quite *fiery*," he said, cracking himself up.

Maddie rolled her eyes. "I can put out the flames one at a time using ultralow frequencies," she explained hurriedly. "Like the bass at a concert. And I can rewire Lexi's speaker to pump them out at a hundred twenty decibels."

"That's loud enough to deafen a yak!" exclaimed Caleb.

"What's with you and yaks?" asked Lexi.

"The other book I was reading was *101 Yak Facts*!" said Caleb. "I can't help it if I have a wide range of interests!"

It wasn't pretty, but Maddie had managed to combine her phone and Lexi's speaker. She turned the volume all the way up, and the walls of the room began to rattle from the powerful sound waves—*BOOM, BOOM, BOOM*.

The closest jet of fire was almost licking Maddie's face. She pointed the speaker right at the nozzle—and the potent vibrations suppressed the fire. *It worked!* She saw her team's disbelief from across the room. "It's blasting away the oxygen between me and the nozzle! The fire needs to breathe oxygen, just like us," she shouted. She moved ahead slowly, holding out Lexi's speaker to blast away any flames that dared try to stop her.

She was nearly free when a pillar of fire behind her rotated toward her. Sensing the flame, Maddie somersaulted forward, finally reaching the far door and escaping the inferno. She wiped the sweat off her forehead. "Thanks for letting me use this," she said, handing

Lexi back her slightly melted speaker.

"That was amazing!" said Lexi. "You just put out a fire with your phone!"

The rest of Maddie's team surrounded her, except for Killian. "That was too cool, Maddie," said Caleb. "Unbelievable."

Maddie felt her body relax. "I kind of can't believe it, either," she said.

She looked back at the burning death trap she'd just escaped. It was the hardest thing she'd ever done. And it was only day one. To survive here, she would need to work like she'd never worked before. Maddie looked at her new teammates, then out the window overlooking Camp Minerva. A world of adventure as a super spy awaited her if she could pass her training.

I can do this, Maddie thought. And surprisingly, a smile formed on her lips. Because for the first time, she finally knew what she was working toward.

CHAPTER 11

Citius altius fortius
Faster, higher, stronger

The next two weeks went by in a blur of hands-on training sessions, lectures on secret knowledge, and surprise off-island excursions. "You cannot learn how to escape from quicksand unless you are dropped in quicksand," Volkov told them during a trip to the Brazilian rain forest.

Enjoying some rare downtime, Maddie, Lexi, and Caleb relaxed at a picnic table near the camp's lake, which was also the site of their next session with Volkov. Maddie was using her phone's 3D software to draw a mock-up of a hoverbike, Caleb was teaching himself ancient Greek, and Lexi was challenging herself to a push-up contest.

Maddie looked up at the clouds. She was sure her

parents would be proud of her for making it this far. Heck, she was pretty darn proud of herself. Lexi must've caught her looking at the sky. "What ya thinking about, Maddie?"

Maddie normally might have told a white lie, but she trusted Lexi and Caleb. "My parents," she said.

"What are they like?" asked Caleb.

"They're brave!" said Maddie. "And smart. They're scientists, too!" Her gaze shifted to the ground. "But they're gone. Missing. Somewhere in the North Pole."

"I'm so sorry," Lexi whispered.

"I guess I'm lucky to have both my parents," said Caleb. "Not that I see them very often."

"Are they, like, world-famous detectives?" guessed Maddie.

Caleb shook his head. "No, no. My father's a diplomat. I was born in St. Louis but he's always traveling to some far-off place. I have to go with him."

"That sounds fun!" said Maddie.

Caleb shook his head. "I've been to six schools in four years on three continents. Not an easy way to make friends."

"You've got friends now," Maddie said. "You just had to join the Illuminati to find anyone cool enough," she added, grinning and gesturing to herself and Lexi.

Caleb laughed. "Yeah, I guess so!"

"You don't have any brothers or sisters, either of you?" asked Lexi, concerned. "I don't know what I'd do without my brothers! I've got four older ones."

"So you're the youngest of five?" asked Caleb.

"Nope!" replied Lexi. "I've also got four younger brothers!"

Maddie tried to imagine having a family that big and shook her head. "Are they all as tough as you?" she asked.

"No," Lexi said sadly. "They're way tougher! I can never live up to the boys!"

"I bet by the end of the summer, you'll be the toughest one," said Maddie. "And besides, I definitely need someone as tough as you to help me get through training."

Before Lexi could reply, they heard Killian come over a hill with Volkov and knew their next session was about to start.

"Excellent work on your marksmanship exam, Recruit Horne," Volkov said to Killian.

"Well, your teaching has been exemplary, Grand Sentinel Volkov," Killian replied.

Lexi rolled her eyes.

What a suck-up, Maddie thought.

The rest of Maddie's training squad arrived, as did TuxBots carrying scuba suits. "Recruits," said Volkov, gesturing to Camp Minerva's lake. "Welcome to Narcissus Lake. This is not just a spot for calm reflection. It is also the world's deepest man-made dive pool at one hundred fifteen feet."

Killian went pale. "This is the dive pool? Come on, we've all heard the rumors: there are piranhas in there!"

Maddie and the other recruits nodded. They'd heard the same rumors.

Volkov went on. "The real danger would be to succumb to your fear. Now watch me carefully," she said as she demonstrated how to put on the scuba gear and attach their air tanks. "If you do this wrong," she warned, "do not count on me to save you." She looked at Maddie with her real eye.

When they were all suited up, Volkov pointed to the pool. "Dive until you see the device," she commanded.

As Maddie prepared to jump in with her team, she noticed something off. Way off. "My tank is only ten percent full!" she yelled to Volkov, who smirked.

"They all are," Volkov explained. "The harder you breathe, the faster you'll use your tank up." Maddie stood frozen. "Best to stay calm. Now dive!"

And Maddie jumped in.

It sort of felt like floating.

As her unit slowly descended, the lake got narrower and narrower. Maddie did her best to control her breathing. But as they went deeper, the light from outside grew weaker and the lake narrowed further into a man-made tunnel. They went down slowly. *What are we looking for exactly?* Maddie asked herself.

They continued to descend until it was as dark above them as it was below. They flipped on their headlamps but could still see only a few inches in front of them. Maddie still had 8 percent oxygen left in her tank, but she wasn't

sure how long she'd be down there. Part of her wanted to
float back up to the top right then, but she didn't want to
leave without finding the "device" Volkov had mentioned.

And then she saw it: at the very bottom of the pool was
a pedestal with lines of red light zigzagging across the surface. The other recruits were wary, but Maddie swam over

and touched it. The red zigzags shot over to her hand, creating an outline of her palm that blinked red. Just then, a hidden roof, 115 feet above them, slid over the top of the lake, trapping Maddie and her entire squad underwater in near-total darkness.

Killian, breathing heavily, swam over to the pedestal, poking and prodding the device. They had no way to communicate, but Killian's glare showed his fear and his anger at Maddie, as if she had somehow caused their situation.

Maddie did her best to assess the device. *Maybe it's a palm-print ID reader?* she thought, but she put her palm on the device again and nothing happened. She looked at her regulator and saw that she only had 5 percent left in her tank.

Suddenly, Sefu and Rolly swam toward her. Or rather, past her. Maddie saw what they were trying to escape from, but it was too late. A swarm of giant piranhas with freakish human teeth suddenly rushed toward Maddie, enveloping her completely. Maddie kicked hard to shake them off, but this only seemed to make it harder to get free. She was trapped!

Then Maddie felt something grab her back. She turned her head—it was Killian, ripping off her oxygen tank. Maddie's eyes widened as Killian's gleamed with greed. He reached for her mouth, and Maddie only had time to take one more big gulp of air before the respirator was tugged away from her. She lunged for Killian, but it was too late. The piranhas swarmed him and disappeared into the darkness.

Maddie was out of air, 115 feet underwater!

Just as she was about to start really panicking, she saw Lexi swim over to her. Lexi took the breathing tube from her mouth and shared it with Maddie. Caleb, seeing what was happening, swam over and gave his tube to Lexi. They cycled the two oxygen tanks among the three of them.

Maddie was furious. And scared. It was like this test was designed to be impossible. She needed to slow her breathing before they all ran out of air. Something suddenly clicked. What if staying calm was the whole point? What if the pedestal wasn't a fingerprint reader at all. . . .

Maddie swam over to the pedestal with Lexi and Caleb in tow. She passed the oxygen tube back to Caleb and reached out to the device. The other recruits gathered and watched as the red lights again formed to Maddie's palm, blinking. But Maddie began to slow her breathing. *Calmer . . . calmer . . .* , she told herself. The seconds ticked by agonizingly as she forced her breathing to slow. *Calmer . . .* Her heart rate slowed, first to her normal rate, then even slower. As she entered a state of total relaxation, almost like she was meditating, the red light around her palm turned green, and the roof above them retracted. Maddie would've sighed if she had any extra air to spare.

After the group safely returned to the surface, Maddie tore off her mask. Volkov watched emotionlessly and gave Maddie a single clap for her efforts. For some reason, Volkov's gaze sent a shiver down Maddie's spine. It was almost as though Volkov had wanted Maddie to fail.

"So it was a heart-rate monitor," said Killian. "A simple solution. I would've figured it out if I wasn't being swarmed by piranhas."

"If you don't need Maddie, then why did you steal her tank?" asked Lexi, angry on Maddie's behalf. "You—*you*—"

"*You scoundrel!*" said Caleb.

"Survival of the fittest," Killian scoffed, taking off the last of his scuba gear and walking away.

"A miracle," said Sefu to himself, "that none of us were eaten by piranhas."

"Not exactly," said Caleb. "You saw their weird, human-like teeth? Those weren't actually piranhas—they're red-bellied pacus. They look like piranhas, but they're vegetarian."

"What a relief," said Lexi. She turned to Maddie. "Amazing thinking down there! You really are a genius!"

Maddie smiled. "I couldn't have done it without you. Or you," she said to Caleb. She finished taking off her gear and ran to hug them both. "Together," she told them both, "there's nothing we can't do."

That night, in her bunk, Maddie thought of Jessica and Jay. She wondered if they missed her. Even though she was having so much fun, she missed them. She missed the evenings watching the Phillies, sharing a bowl of popcorn, and laughing every time Jay yelled at the TV. She missed

Jessica braiding her hair before school. She even sometimes missed the lumpy orange couch she slept on, even though it was definitely not as comfortable as her ergonomic foam mattress that floated above Lexi's, like a magnetic bunk bed.

Her Illuminati-issued sleeping bag, a navy-blue silk stitched with a pattern of golden triangles, was much more luxurious than the floral polyester comforter she had at home. But still, she missed that old couch, with its lumps and the spring that poked her in the back sometimes. There was something nice about knowing that the only family she had in the world, Jessica and Jay, were just in the next room.

Before she fell asleep, she decided to write them a postcard. Volkov encouraged recruits to write to their families and friends back home, to keep up the cover story that they were at an exceptional summer camp, learning tech skills and having wholesome outdoor fun. Of course, Camp Minerva had agents who read each letter, destroying ones that gave away too many details or weren't convincing enough. Maddie learned to be fairly vague in her notes, but she always signed her name with *X*s and *O*s to express her love. The postcards and envelopes they were given to use were already stamped with *Camp Minerva* and a return address somewhere in Ohio, so no one could tell they were really at a top secret Illuminati training facility on a tropical island in the middle of the ocean.

But they rarely got letters from home. Volkov said it was because the Illuminati didn't want recruits being distracted by feelings of homesickness and wanted them to bond with each other. Maddie supposed that made sense. Still, as her head hit her pillow that night, she couldn't help but think about Jay and Jessica and whether or not they had gotten a new microwave.

CHAPTER 12

Dulce periculum.

Danger is sweet.

As the weeks passed, Maddie noticed fewer and fewer recruits in the Chow Hall each morning. The recruits who stayed were changing, too, including their training unit. Caleb had found some confidence and began walking with his chin up instead of looking at the ground, and Lexi's arm muscles were getting even more defined. Maddie felt stronger herself, too. Her legs were often sore from all the training they did, and her core was now strong from the acrobatic airborne somersault workshop she'd just completed.

"A lot of people are dropping out," said Lexi.

"Or failing out," said Caleb.

"Not me!" said Lexi, pulling up her holographic schedule on her S.M.A.R.T.W.A.T.C.H., which was short for Silicon Multiphase Activity Record Tracking, Wrist-bound, Algorithm-processing, Timekeeping, and Computing Hologram. Maddie did the same.

"I've got Symbology and Mythology," said Maddie.

"I'm in a safecracking course later," said Lexi. "I hope there are explosions!"

Maddie saw her final class after an open lab session and gave a little squeal of delight: "Special Assembly: Atlantis—Fact vs. Fiction!"

"And then I have sewing lessons," said Lexi.

Maddie nearly spat out her milk. "Sewing lessons?"

Lexi looked hurt. "It's medicinal sewing with quick-heal gel stitches!" she explained. "And so what if I know how to do regular sewing, too?!"

"You're right," said Maddie. "I'm sorry."

Lexi smiled. "It's okay!" she said.

Rolly took one of the table's open seats. He looked ill.

"Rolly, I mean this as politely as possible," said Caleb. "But you look terrible."

Rolly nodded slowly. "I had poison immunity training last night," he said woozily, in the voice of an old Italian count. "I never would have signed up if I'd known the way to become immune was just to slowly eat a bunch of poison!"

Maddie suppressed a smile.

"I think I need a nap," said Rolly, in a deep southern

drawl, as he passed out in his chair.

Maddie looked over at Caleb, who looked sleepy, his eyes far less alert than normal.

"Ask me anything," he said slowly.

"Okay . . . ," said a weirded-out Maddie. "What's two plus two?"

"Excellent question. My auntie Rebecca is terrified of tinfoil. She spends her time making hand-crafted wind chimes out of driftwood and macaroni!"

Maddie stared at Caleb blankly. "The answer I was looking for was 'four.'"

Caleb smiled. "I know. I was testing myself—a visiting MI6 agent just taught me how to lie through truth serum. I still have some in my system. Since you can't lie, the trick is to tell the truth about something else."

"Smart," said Maddie. "So what do you really think of Auntie Rebecca's wind chimes?" she asked, teasing her friend.

"They're . . . well, she . . . My auntie Rebecca speaks over a hundred languages, including sixteen she made up herself, so, um, who am I to judge?"

Maddie giggled and was about to zip out the door to her first class when a TuxBot rolled up—holding a letter from home. Maddie tore into it immediately.

Dear Maddie,

We miss you! I'm glad to hear that you're making lots

of new friends and impressing everyone with your inven-
tions. Remember how I used to always say that it was
like you were always on a different frequency than most
other people? I hope that Lexi and Caleb are on your
frequency.

We love you!

Jessica

PS—Jay won a contest on LyonCorp and they mailed
him fifty microwaves! He had so many that he started
giving them away. Everybody's calling him Jay the
Microwave Man now!

Maddie chuckled, imagining Jessica and Jay's apartment filled to the ceiling with microwaves. *At least he'll never bug me about that again!* she thought. She smiled, thinking about her family enjoying their summer as much as she was.

Maddie, Caleb, and Lexi finished their breakfast. According to Maddie's S.M.A.R.T.W.A.T.C.H., they had fifteen minutes before their morning classes. They left the Chow Hall (and a sleeping Rolly) and settled under the shade of a wide oak tree.

Maddie took a second to admire her Illuminati-issued uniform: an electric-blue hoodie with matching pants and electric-blue-and-yellow sneakers. Although it looked like everyday athleisure, the fabric was actually a high-tech, stretchy, sweat-wicking, odor-eliminating, stain-repelling material that wouldn't rip, burn, or get moth holes.

Caleb looked at his daily schedule and groaned. "I'm spending all day in classes with Volkov."

"Ooh," said Lexi and Maddie together. "That's rough," added Lexi.

"Is it just me," asked Maddie, "or does Volkov hate everyone not named Killian?"

"And Killian's rotten like a cucumber left in the sun!" said Lexi.

Caleb nodded. "There's just something off about Volkov," he said. "I can't quite put my finger on it. . . ." Before he could finish his thought, the tree they were sitting under started rumbling. Maddie, Caleb, and Lexi quickly scooted a few feet away, then watched in shock as the tree bark spread open, revealing a metal door. The door opened with a swoosh—and there stood Volkov, talking into her S.M.A.R.T.W.A.T.C.H. in hushed tones.

"Obscuritas will strike soon," said Volkov. "And I will be ready." She looked up and spotted her trainees, her jeweled eye turning an angry red. "Get. To. Class," she commanded them.

Maddie and friends ran to the Obelisk without looking back. *If Volkov didn't have it out for us before, she definitely does now,* Maddie thought.

"What's Obscuritas?" asked Lexi when they were out of earshot.

"No idea," said Caleb. "But it didn't seem like she was happy we overheard her talking about it."

"Nope, definitely not," agreed Lexi.

At the entrance to the Illuminati's worldwide HQ, Maddie looked at Caleb and Lexi. "Whatever Volkov's planning, it seems like something big. So we'd better be ready. For anything."

CHAPTER 13

Acta non verba

Deeds, not words

The next morning, Maddie bolted awake. She smelled that something was off before she saw anything. The air was drier than the island's. More stale. And it was louder. Way louder.

Wee-ooh! Wee-ooh!

"Move it, pal!"

"Hot dogs! Hot dogs here!"

HONK! HONK! HONK!

Maddie opened her eyes and looked up. The sun was above her, but it was hidden behind tall skyscrapers and impossibly huge video-billboards showing ads for the latest fashions and films. Hundreds of strangers rushed past her, speaking languages from all over the world. *Tourists*, she realized. Maddie rubbed her eyes and noticed she'd been asleep on a sidewalk bench, crammed between Caleb and Lexi, who were just waking up, too.

"Ugh," said Caleb, rubbing his back. "Why does my bunk bed feel like a metal bench?"

"Turn down the radio, Maddie," said Lexi, her pink sleep mask still covering her eyes. "I wanna snooze."

"Guys . . . we're not on the island anymore," said Maddie. "I think . . . I think we're in Times Square, New York City."

Lexi and Caleb shot upright. The flickering lights and scrolling news tickers, the vacationers shrieking with excitement, running and snapping photos all around them—it was enough to shock even the sleepiest recruit to full attention.

Caleb leaped up, bumping into a street performer dressed in a sooty puppet costume. "How did we get here?" Caleb asked, his mind racing. His eyes darted every which way toward any possible clues.

Lexi was nearly hyperventilating. "Stay calm," she said, not following her own advice. "We just have to STAY CALM!"

Maddie stood up and put a hand on Lexi's shoulder. "It's okay," she said, but her brain was bubbling over with questions she couldn't answer. *Who brought us here? And how will we get home? What is going on?* "I have the Obelisk's support number in my phone," she said. "Let's just—" Maddie stuck her hands in her pockets and froze. She wasn't in her Illuminati pajamas anymore, but in her athletic training gear. So were Lexi and Caleb. They blended in seamlessly with the crowd.

All three of them checked their pockets and made the

same discovery: "No phones. No ID. And no money," said Maddie. Even their S.M.A.R.T.W.A.T.C.H.es were missing.

"The last thing I remember is attending morning classes," said Caleb.

"Same," said Maddie. "Then someone must've knocked us out or used a memory-erasing ray on us before dropping us here."

"I always wanted to visit New York City, but not like this!" said Lexi, with a quiver in her voice. "How can we do anything without any money?"

"Or our phones!" said Caleb, starting to hyperventilate.

"We'll figure this out," said Maddie. She looked around, taking in her surroundings. *What is really going on?* she thought. Suddenly, an idea occurred to her. "Wait a second!" she said. "This whole thing is probably just a training exercise!"

"Of course!" Lexi said. "Just because we're not in the middle of a desert or jungle doesn't mean we don't have the skills to handle this."

"New York City *is* a uniquely challenging environment," Caleb mused. "After all, if you can make it here, you can make it anywhere."

All of a sudden, a stranger in a dark green overcoat bumped into Maddie, hard, dropping his phone on the ground. Caleb picked it up as the man disappeared into the crowd. Maddie called after him, "Sir! You dropped your phone!" She took a step forward when Caleb stopped her. His normal *I know everything* expression had given way to a look of worry Maddie hadn't seen on him before.

"Maddie," Caleb said, looking down at an image on the stranger's phone. "I don't think this is a training exercise." He handed her the phone. Somehow, its screen was displaying a message for Maddie in glowing red letters: Hello, Maddie. You have until 3 p.m. to save them. Maddie scrolled down to a photo and screamed. The photo showed Jessica and Jay, tied with thick ropes to some very uncomfortable-looking wooden chairs. They looked scared. She couldn't tell where the picture had been taken. But from the lack of light or windows, it appeared to be a dingy basement.

What have I done? thought Maddie. Someone was trying to hurt her family. But who? With a pit in her stomach, she thought back to Volkov's words from the day before. She'd said that Obscuritas would strike soon. Could this be it? Could Volkov be in on it?

The phone buzzed and a message for Caleb appeared, replacing Maddie's message: Hello, Caleb. You have until 3 p.m. to save her. A photo of a woman with dark brown skin and a kind smile appeared. "Auntie Rebecca!" yelled Caleb.

The phone buzzed again. Maddie's heart sank, knowing the message had horrible news for her other friend. Hello, Lexi. You have until 3 p.m. to save them. The photo was of two athletic tween boys, twins, tied to chairs in a dark basement. "Andy and Andrew!" cried Lexi. "My baby brothers."

"*Baby* brothers?" said Caleb. "They're huge!"

"We'll save them!" said Maddie. "I don't know who's taken our families or why." Maddie glanced at one of the electronic news tickers on the side of a building. "But it's only ten a.m. We have five hours to find them. And we will!"

Too bad I have absolutely no idea how, she worried.

Lexi wiped her eyes. "I'm with you, Maddie. Caleb, I'm sorry about your aunt," she said. Caleb steadied his breath and nodded.

"Thanks," he said. "If we work together, I know we can find them."

Lexi pointed to the phone, still in Maddie's hands. "Maybe there's a clue in there! Maddie, can't you, like, reverse engineer it or something to figure out where those photos were taken?"

"Yes!" Maddie said, tapping away excitedly. Lexi watched over her shoulder as Caleb wandered a few feet away. "Darn it," said Maddie. "Whoever sent those messages knew what they were doing." She dove into the phone's hidden settings menu. "The GPS metadata is scrambled. But I can try something else."

Something caught Caleb's eye. "Hey, Maddie . . . ," he said, too quietly.

"One sec," said Maddie. "I think I'm close to finding a clue. I can triangulate cell tower data and—"

"Maddie," said Caleb. "I think our next clue found us."

Maddie looked up, and Caleb pointed to one of the scrolling news feeds on a massive building. In red letters, a handful of stories scrolled by: *GRIDLOCK IN WASHINGTON; STOCK MARKET UNREST; GLOBAL TEMPERATURE AT ALL-TIME HIGH.*

"Which one is supposed to be a clue?" asked Lexi.

"Trust me, you'll see it," said Caleb. Maddie gasped as the headline appeared: *MADDIE, CALEB, LEXI: THIS GARDEN HAS A SECRET. ONLY WATER CAN BURN IT.*

"Yes!" Lexi shouted. "Great work, Caleb!"

Caleb shrugged. "All I've done so far is find a message written in huge, blinking letters that was projected literally right in front of me."

"What kind of garden is burned by water?" Maddie asked. "Plants love water, so . . . A rock garden? A sculpture garden?"

"Yeah, but rocks and sculptures don't get burned by water, either," said Lexi.

"True," said Maddie.

Caleb's eyes started darting around, like they were peering inside the farthest corners of his brain.

"A garden with a secret . . . ," said Maddie. "Maybe that means the garden *is* the secret, like it's hidden somewhere? But how can you burn it?"

Caleb started thinking out loud. "A secret garden . . . burn it . . . burn it . . *Burnett* . . . That's it!" he shouted. "Central Park! We have to get to Central Park. Now!"

Caleb took off, speed-walking through the throngs of tourists and Times Square characters. Maddie and Lexi followed.

"Why Central Park?" asked Maddie.

"In Central Park, there's a fountain dedicated to the author of the book *The Secret Garden*," said Caleb.

"Who's that?" asked Lexi.

"Frances Hodgson Burnett!" said Caleb.

Maddie high-fived him. "Yes!"

"Now that's great work," said Lexi. "But one problem: How are we going to get there?"

"Run?" offered Maddie. "We don't have time to spare."

"Tour starts in one minute!" yelled a man in a red windbreaker standing next to a double-decker bus. "One bus ride takes you to all the sights! Hop on and hop off wherever you want! First stop: Central Park!"

"Let's go!" said Maddie.

Lexi stopped. "But we can't pay—"

"Just stick close to me," said Maddie.

Maddie, Lexi, and Caleb squeezed into a group of kids waiting to board the bus. The tour guide in the red windbreaker patted his gut with his clipboard as he spoke to the group's chaperone. "Okay, pal, you got fifteen riders here? Step on and I'll count ya off." As the kids in the group started boarding, the man counted to himself: "One . . . two . . . three . . . four . . ."

"Eight!" squawked Maddie into her hand.

"Aw, jeez," said the man in the windbreaker. "I lost count. Uh . . . five . . . six . . ."

"Thirteen!" coughed Caleb under his breath.

"Um, fourteen," said the tour guide. "No, I mean, nine—"

"Seven!" said Lexi.

The guy in the windbreaker nearly dropped his clipboard. "Whatever . . . Everybody aboard!" he grumbled. Maddie, Lexi, and Caleb climbed inside, staying just close enough to the chaperoned group to avoid suspicion. "Next stop, Central Park," said the tour guide over the bus's loudspeaker.

Caleb turned to Maddie and Lexi. "What do you think we'll find at Burnett Fountain?"

"I don't know," said Maddie. "But I won't stop until our families are safe."

CHAPTER 14

Faber est suae quisque fortunae.
Every man is the maker of his own fortune.

The bus pulled into a busy traffic circle. "Central Park, ladies and gents," said the tour guide in the red wind-breaker. Maddie, Caleb, and Lexi jumped off and ran past a statue of Columbus into the park's southwest entrance.

"Where's that fountain?" asked Maddie.

"The northeast corner of the park," said Caleb.

"So, the exact opposite of where we are," said Lexi with a frown.

"Not the *exact* opposite," replied Caleb. "The fountain's at 104th Street and we're at 59th, so—"

"So we're still forty-five blocks away!" said Maddie. She took a deep breath, and then all three of them took off running into the park at full speed.

"Pardon me!"

"Sorry!"

"Sorry about this! Excuse us!"

Maddie called out apologies as the trio bobbed and weaved through the power-walking retirees, the Frisbee-chasing dogs, and the assorted world travelers enjoying the crowded park. They goose-stepped through a great lawn covered in goose droppings, cut through a crafting circle on a rocky outcropping, and hustled through the outfield of half a dozen softball games.

Maddie swerved left at a fork in the road, under a small bridge where a saxophone player was firing off solos. Off the path to her right, a seventy-foot-tall stone pillar stood out, engraved with faded Egyptian hieroglyphics—and metallic crab pincers sticking out of the base at all four corners. "Hey, that looks just like the Obelisk at Camp Minerva. What the . . . ?"

"It's called Cleopatra's Needle," said a winded Caleb. "Built in 1475 BCE. Ancient Egypt."

Maddie was stunned. "What's it doing here?"

Lexi ran past them. "No time for a history lesson! We've got families to save," she said. The longer, blue half of her hair whipped in the wind. Maddie picked up her pace to match.

Moments later, they came to a humongous reservoir as wide as the entire park.

"Wait!" Caleb begged. "I just have to catch my breath." He took off his glasses to wipe the sweat off them.

"It's only been twenty blocks," said Lexi. "We have to keep going."

"It's been twenty-seven blocks!" Caleb lamented.

"I could carry you piggyback-style," Lexi offered, half seriously.

Caleb shot her an insecure look. "No way."

Maddie looked at him. "You okay?" she asked. She could see he was even more winded than he let on. "We really need you, Caleb." He saw the concern in her eyes and nodded.

"Race you there," he said as he sprinted onto the path around the reservoir.

Several minutes later, they arrived at Burnett Fountain.

The fountain truly was like a secret garden, a serene park-within-a-park, surrounded on all sides by large floral displays. In the center was a small reflecting pool, with a bronze statue of two children, a boy and a girl, at its base. The figure of the girl held a bowl that spurted out water at odd intervals: *Splish-splish-splish-splish-SPLASH!*

"Caleb," said Maddie, "are you sure this is the place?"

Caleb looked concerned. "I thought so. But I don't see anything," he said. Maddie could see the doubt creeping onto his face. She was pretty sure she had the same look on her face.

There's got to be a clue here! Maddie thought. "Let's all look around. In every nook and cranny," she said. "There's got to be something we're missing." She started poking and prodding the statues, feeling for hidden switches. Lexi tried to lift the stone benches off the ground. Then she stepped into the reflecting pool, looking for anything that could help them. Caleb stayed put—and Maddie noticed his eyes weren't darting around the way they usually did when he was deep in thought. *If Caleb can't spot anything,* Maddie thought, *maybe it is time to give up.*

"Caleb, any thoughts?" Maddie asked. *Splish-splish-splish, SPLASH!* The sound was starting to get on her nerves.

"None," Caleb said, defeated.

"We could really use some help looking for clues," said Lexi.

"How can I find clues when I don't even see a puzzle!" snapped Caleb. "Show me a puzzle, and I'll solve it! But this . . ." He seemed scared. Maddie understood why. "Someone kidnapped my auntie Rebecca! And we're just running around a park! She could already be . . ." Caleb crumpled onto a bench, too scared to say just how scared he was.

Maddie sat beside him. "I understand," she said. "They've got my family, too. And Lexi's." Caleb nodded. "But that's not a reason to give up. That's the reason we have to keep going."

Splish-splish-splish, SPLASH!

"Gosh, that splashing is so loud. It's hard to concentrate. I need to think," Maddie said.

Splish-splish-splish, SPLASH!

"That's it!" cried Caleb.

"What's it?" said Maddie.

"Hold on, I need to listen," said Caleb. He ran over to the fountain's jet.

Splish-splish-splish!

Splish-splish-splish-splish-SPLASH!

Splish-splish-splish, SPLASH!

Splish-splish-splish, SPLASH!

"It's Morse code!" exclaimed Caleb. He nearly jumped up and down with glee. "The water—it's a pattern! There was a puzzle in front of us the whole time!"

They all listened again.

"Yes! What's it saying?" asked Lexi.

Caleb tapped his foot in time with the spurts as he deciphered the code. "It's repeating something: *S 4 S T S T*," he said.

Maddie repeated the code, trying to make sense of it. "*S 4 S T S T*."

Caleb perked up. "A single *S* is usually short for 'south.' So—of course!—'South Four' and '*ST*' is street! That's South Fourth Street!"

Maddie looked perplexed. "But doesn't the code end with '*ST ST*'? So it's South Fourth Street . . . Street?"

Caleb brightened. "*ST* stands for station! It's South Fourth Street Station! A subway stop!"

"Let's go!" said Lexi, jumping out of the reflecting pool.

Maddie pulled out the phone the stranger had dropped and opened the map app. Then she let out a disappointed sigh. "Except, according to this, there is no South Fourth Street Station."

Caleb dusted some dirt off his jacket. "Not in Manhattan," he said confidently. "But there is a South Fourth Street Station in Brooklyn." He looked sideways. "Sort of."

"Meaning?" asked Maddie.

"The station started to be built in 1929, but it was never finished and the project was abandoned before it ever opened. So it's just a—"

"A dark, empty basement covered in graffiti and spiderwebs?" said Maddie.

"That must be where they're keeping Andrew and Andy!" said Lexi.

Maddie checked the phone.

It was nearly noon. Only three hours left to save Jessica and Jay.

You got this, Maddie said to herself. She hoped that believing it would make it true. "Brooklyn, here we come."

CHAPTER 15

Non ducor, duco.
I am not led, I lead.

Maddie's fingers fired away on the stranger's map app, looking for the best route.

"Isn't Brooklyn across, like, an ocean?" asked Lexi.

"The East River," replied Caleb.

"All right! I wouldn't say no to a vigorous swim," said Lexi.

"I would," Caleb mumbled.

Maddie checked the phone. "We're just a couple blocks from the subway. We can take it all the way to the abandoned South Fourth Street Station. But it'll take us an hour to get there."

"How are we going to pay for subway tickets?" asked Caleb.

Maddie was already heading out of the park to the 103rd Street subway stop. "I have a plan!" she said.

The nearby subway station was mostly empty. A serious-looking Metropolitan Transportation Authority officer paced the waiting area.

"Getting through the turnstiles and onto the train without getting caught won't be easy," said Caleb.

"But we're agents of the Illuminati—almost. This is what we do!" said Maddie. She nudged Caleb and Lexi toward a MetroCard vending machine. "Can you please stand between me and that surveillance camera?" she asked Lexi and Caleb quietly.

Maddie manipulated the touch screen with rapidly tapping fingertips. "Let me just bypass the main screen and hack in through the backdoor. . . ." She glanced around to see if anyone noticed what she was doing. But no one did—the few people in the station barely looked up from their phones as they waited for the train. Maddie continued tapping and swiping through lines of code. "Almost there . . . just need to flip this input and . . . We're good!"

The MTA machine beeped and spat out three yellow MetroCards. "These should have unlimited rides for today," said Maddie. "But if they don't work at the turnstiles, we're going to have to figure out something else—or jump over them!"

"I can clear this, easy as cucumber pie!" said Lexi.

"Uh, cool it on the jumping talk," whispered Caleb. He

nodded his head at the MTA officer, who was standing by the subway entrance, just waiting for someone to cause trouble.

The kids walked up to the turnstiles, where they had to swipe their MetroCards. *Click!*—

Lexi's worked! *Click!*—Caleb's worked! They hurried through the turnstiles to the other side of the heavy metal gate. *Beep!!!*—Maddie's did not work. The turnstile bar knocked into her stomach, hard.

Oof, she thought. *I guess I screwed this one up.*

"Maddie, you good?" asked Lexi.

Maddie looked at the display screen. *Swipe Again at This Turnstile.*

She mustered her courage and swiped again.

Beep!!!— *Swipe Again at This Turnstile.*

"Maddie?" asked Caleb nervously.

Maddie began to sweat as the station started to rumble with an incoming train. The MTA security guard looked her way. *Can he tell I'm using a hacked card?* she wondered. She wiped her hands on her pants and tried the card again, to no avail. "Come on, come on," Maddie whispered to herself.

"Maddie, pick up the pace," said Lexi. "The train's almost here!"

The MTA officer started walking closer to Maddie. *I can't get caught now!* Had she accidentally set off some sort of alarm? She swiped desperately one more time.

Click!—and she was through! Without a backward

107

glance, Maddie joined Lexi and Caleb, and they quickly wove through a dense crowd and hopped onto a Brooklyn-bound train.

Nearly fifty minutes later, they climbed up the subway steps and found themselves in Brooklyn, in the ultrahip neighborhood of Williamsburg. They hustled the last few blocks to their destination, but when they arrived, there was no sign of the abandoned South 4th Street Station.

"I don't know why I was hoping there'd be a big sign saying 'Top Secret Hidden Subway Station This Way,'" said Maddie, glancing around the residential street. It was full of glass-walled, modern-looking condos, busy Laundromats, and hip coffee shops with Swedish-sounding names. The sidewalk was crowded with people with whimsical hair colors, wearing serious-looking black clothing. A woman in a sundress walking a very fluffy Pomeranian stared at Maddie, Lexi, and Caleb, as if she had never seen anyone without any tattoos before. "It's all underground—we should almost be standing on top of it right now," said Caleb, trying to measure out coordinates with the length of his shadow.

"Actually, we are," said Lexi as she stepped into the street.

"Lexi!" Maddie and Caleb yelled as a yellow taxi swerved to avoid her. Lexi stopped and began to wipe the grime off a manhole cover.

"Oh yeah!" shouted Lexi.

Hidden in plain sight was the strangest manhole cover

Maddie had ever seen: it was golden-colored, engraved with intertwined symbols she didn't recognize from any of her Illuminati symbology classes. But there, in the center, was the now-familiar golden triangle.

"Whoa," said Caleb.

Maddie checked the phone the stranger had dropped. *Only two hours left to save our families,* she thought.

"That's our way in," she said. "Nice work, Lexi!"

Lexi grunted and pried the solid metal cover away, revealing a ladder to the darkness below.

Caleb took a deep breath. "It's really dark."

"Nothing ventured, nothing gained!" said Maddie, mimicking Volkov's strong Eastern European accent.

Lexi bravely climbed down first. Maddie and Caleb followed. They felt a little weird about leaving a gaping hole in the middle of a Brooklyn street, but there was no time for covering their tracks.

At the bottom of the ladder, Maddie turned on the phone's flashlight.

"Jessica? Jay?" she called out.

The abandoned South 4th Street Station was enormous and empty, with a slightly wet floor and a closed-up, musty smell. Rusty, unlaid pieces of track lurked in shadowy piles by the walls. Empty benches gathered thick layers of dust. Graffiti artists had covered the walls with beautiful, colorful murals that only the most daring, adventurous New Yorkers would ever see. Maddie tried to step quietly, but her careful footsteps caused booming echoes anyway.

"Where do we go now?" Caleb whispered.

Maddie pointed the phone's flashlight toward a darkened corner and spotted an old subway car. "This way." Walking closer, she noticed the car had room for only one or two people—the rest of the car was taken up by a huge 1960s-style computer, complete with space for tape loops and paper punch cards. At the top, the machine was labeled *Checkers-Playing Supercomputer.*

"Checkers?" Maddie said to herself.

The rest of the tracks were home to subway cars similarly stuffed with old-school tech: bulky video monitors playing static on an endless loop, wall-sized cryogenic freezers, and bus-sized rocket boosters.

"This must've been extremely futuristic technology for its time," Maddie said as Caleb and Lexi caught up to her. She pointed to the rocket boosters. "Now, Zander Lyon wears two of those strapped to his feet when he skydives."

"Maddie, try not to get sucked in by all the old-timey tech," said Caleb. "We're on a deadline."

"Right." Time was ticking down. *Two hours left to find Jessica and Jay.*

Maddie noticed a row of arches on the other side of the station. One was covered up by thin plywood. "Let's check over there," she said. As they climbed down onto the tracks and back up the other side, Maddie saw the thinnest ray of light from behind the sealed arch. "Think we can get through there?" she asked.

Lexi laughed. "Oh yeah. And it'll be fun, too," she said, before karate-kicking the wall. The plywood barrier smashed apart with a cloud of sawdust and a loud *crack!* Caleb high-fived Lexi, who took an elegant bow. Maddie pointed the phone's flashlight into the stone-walled nook of a room. She couldn't quite make out what was inside.

"Treasure?" said Lexi.

"No," said Maddie. "Keys." The room was filled with hundreds and hundreds of keys, in all shapes and sizes. Keys hanging from the walls and ceiling, in piles on small tables, even spilling out of chests on the ground. A single lit candle gave the room an eerie glow.

"This place is, um, super-creepy, right?" asked Lexi.

"On a creepiness scale from one to ten, this place gets a fifteen," said Caleb. "Anyone see any clues?"

Maddie shivered, then pointed to graffiti on the wall: *Play? Choose a key.*

Caleb took a step forward into the room as Maddie continued. "Watch out for booby traps—" But her warning came too late. A transparent box dropped from the ceiling, trapping Caleb inside with a loud clang. He banged on the heavy glass, which barely moved.

"Caleb!" Maddie cried.

"—!" yelled Caleb.

"It's soundproof!" said Maddie. "Don't worry, Caleb! We'll get you out! We just have to find the right key!" She and Lexi started grabbing every key they saw.

"It could be any one of these!" said Lexi as she picked up a large key shaped like a dragon midflight.

Maddie climbed onto a small table and read the inscription on a large key hanging from the ceiling. "This one's the key to the city of Akron, Ohio!" She glanced back at Caleb, who had started looking pale inside the glass cage. He pointed to his throat, then slumped over. "He's running out of oxygen!" Maddie searched furiously for a key that would help them.

Lexi held an armful of keys: Victorian skeleton keys, wooden keys, an ivory key with an emerald handle. Maddie saw that Caleb's face was starting to turn blue. "I don't even see a keyhole!" cried Lexi.

She's right, Maddie realized. *So it's got to be some other type of key!* "It's not a real key!" she shouted. "It's a puzzle!"

Using his last bit of air, Caleb stood ramrod straight and opened his mouth wide, holding an imaginary microphone in one hand and gesturing wildly with the other.

"What is he doing?" Lexi asked.

"Is he singing?" Maddie wondered aloud. "We can't hear you!" Caleb's eyes fluttered and he slumped back to the ground. Maddie knew he had only a few seconds left before he'd be totally out of air.

She looked back at the graffiti: *Play? Choose a key.* Then it all clicked. "Lexi, the sign doesn't mean choose a key. It means *sing* the key of A! That's why Caleb was singing!"

"AaaAAaaaAAAA!" Maddie shout-sang. Caleb's eyes closed.

"What are you doing?" asked Lexi.

"The A key! The musical key of A! That's the answer! But I don't know how to sing!" cried Maddie.

Lexi stepped next to the glass cage. "I got this." She cleared her throat, took a deep breath, and then: "AaaaAAAAAA!" In an instant, her pitch-perfect voice shattered the glass cell. Caleb gasped for breath as glass shards tumbled around him like a pile of hail.

Maddie and Lexi rushed to Caleb's side. "Are you all right?" Maddie asked. Still catching his breath, Caleb gave a thumbs-up. "If you hadn't started singing," Maddie said to him, "I never would've figured it out." Caleb got up and silently hugged them both.

"Lexi, that was amazing!" he finally said. "How did you do that?"

Lexi shrugged, embarrassed. "Let's just say my parents made me try out a whole lot of different after-school activities before they finally let me take judo."

Maddie examined the shards that had made up the glass cage. "It must be specially formulated to be extra strong but to crack immediately when a particular resonant tone is played. Unbelievably cool."

Caleb rolled his eyes at Maddie's curiosity. "It was a thrill to almost die in such a scientifically ingenious way," he said.

Maddie smiled at him, brushing away a shard of glass that had gotten stuck in his hair. But then she looked around, disappointed.

"We saved him," said Lexi. "What's the problem?"

Maddie sighed. "Yeah, but we're still no closer to finding our families."

"Not exactly," said Caleb. "There was a message for us playing inside that box."

Maddie perked up. Whoever was doing this, they had a knack for technology. *Well, I have that too,* she thought. She was more determined than ever. They hadn't saved Jessica and Jay yet, but Maddie knew that they could.

There's nothing that can stop us when we're working together, she thought.

"So where to?" Lexi asked Caleb.

"I'll explain on the way," he said. "Whoever is doing this, they said they're waiting for us at the Statue of Liberty."

CHAPTER 16

Timendi causa est nescire.
Ignorance is the cause of fear.

The kids climbed back out of the abandoned subway station, slid the golden manhole cover back to where it had been, and raced to an actual, working subway station. Luckily, Maddie's hacked MetroCards worked again, and they hopped the first train that arrived, then transferred to another subway to get to lower Manhattan.

"Wouldn't it be faster just to swim?" Lexi asked, rolling her shoulders, looking uncomfortable in the subway car, squashed between an older woman in five strands of pearls reading a book entitled *Secrets of the Illuminati, Vol. 1* and a man eating an aromatic meatball sub.

Maddie nudged Caleb, nodding her head at the title of the book the older woman was reading. She waggled her eyebrows. "I wonder what she'd do if she knew real Illuminati agents were riding the subway right next to her!" Maddie whispered.

"Actually, *Secrets of the Illuminati, Volume Two* is much more accurate," Caleb said, a little too loudly. "I read all four volumes."

"Shhhh!" Maddie said.

Just then, the subway screeched to a halt. "It's our stop!" Caleb cried, and they dashed out and up the stairs. They found themselves in Battery Park, a concrete expanse with sections of grass and trees, facing the slate-gray Hudson River. The park was filled with tourists, hot dog stands, and kiosks selling trinkets and Statue of Liberty headbands made of green foam.

"Anyone see a ticket machine we can hack?" asked Maddie.

"Just a regular, ticket-selling human," said Lexi. "And we've still got no money."

"Maybe it's time for a little more Illuminati Improvisation 101," suggested Caleb.

Maddie nodded. Time was running out. So they huddled together, sidling up to a visiting school group that looked to be about their ages. They tried to blend into the center of the crowd of laughing, shouting kids and snuck aboard the ferry to Liberty Island.

"Can't this boat go any faster?" asked a worried Maddie. She looked at the phone. *Two forty-five,* she thought. *Only fifteen minutes left to save our families.*

"I still think we should've swam," said Lexi.

"Technically, it would've taken us longer to swim, factoring in water currents and river traffic," Caleb said, trying to be reassuring. "But did I mention I get seasick?" he said, his face green. He started slow, deep breathing.

"What's our plan once we get to Liberty Island?" asked Lexi.

"I don't know," admitted Maddie. "I just hope we'll see what to do when we get there."

Lexi looked worried. "Do you think Andy and Andrew are okay?" she asked.

Lexi was the toughest person Maddie had ever met. *She's just as scared as I am*, Maddie realized. "We'll get to them in time. I know it," she told her friend. *I hope.* "Caleb, you're sure we're supposed to go to the Statue of Liberty?" Maddie checked the phone again: *2:48*.

"Definitely," replied the young sleuth in between his deep breathing. "When I was stuck in that cage, the message kept repeating: 'Before a giant's welcome, rest deeply.'"

"That doesn't sound like 'Statue of Liberty' to me," said Lexi.

"Another puzzle," said Caleb.

"Rest deeply?" asked Lexi. "Like, take a nap?"

2:49.

"This one was actually kind of simple," said Caleb, with a hint of a smile. "'Rest deeply' is the big clue: Liberty Island was actually called Bedloe's Island until 1956."

"Ohhh. Bed low, aka 'rest deeply,'" said Maddie.

"Exactly," said Caleb. "And the Statue of Liberty herself is the most welcoming giant I know."

"I'm glad you're here, Caleb," said Lexi. "Except for the whole kidnapping-your-aunt thing! I'm sorry you have to deal with that part."

Caleb nodded and took another deep breath. "We're in this together."

As they got closer to the island, the immense size of Lady Liberty finally dawned on them. Her stoic, reassuring face was so high up, even the seagulls didn't dare fly up there.

With a powerful *thud*, the ferry docked at Liberty Island. "Let's go!" cried Maddie. Pushing her way through the crowd, she ran off the boat and looked around. *Where could Jessica and Jay be hidden?* she asked herself. *You have to think! The basement of the visitors' center? Deep below that huge stone pedestal?* She looked at the phone.

2:54.

Caleb and Lexi came up behind her. "We should split up to cover more ground," said Caleb.

Maddie gazed up at the immense statue, taking in all 305 feet of Lady Liberty, from tip to torch. *Of course,* she realized. "No," she said boldly. "We're going all the way up to the top. That's where our families are."

"Are you sure?" asked Lexi.

"That's a public place," said Caleb. "It's hardly a dingy basement—"

"I'm sure," said Maddie. She pointed to the torch. "Don't you remember?" she said. "The light always shows the way."

Caleb and Lexi smiled.

No other convincing was necessary. The trio ran to the statue's base and kept running once inside.

"Last tour of the day has already ended," mumbled a seated security guard, but they ran past, into the stairwell.

They paused just a moment to look up. And up, and up. Up the stairs toward their families.

2:56.

"Only three hundred fifty-four steps. No problem," said Caleb as they careened up the winding metal staircase. Halfway up, Lexi overtook Maddie. Maddie wanted to stop and catch her breath, but the thought of Jessica and Jay pushed her onward.

2:57.

As they ran, Maddie's lungs started to burn. *You can save them!* she told herself. *Push!* She pumped her legs and ran fast enough to overtake Lexi.

2:58.

Maddie heard a commotion above them. *The crown! We're so close!* Her legs felt like pudding. She was covered in sweat, head to toe. Every muscle in her body screamed, *GIVE UP NOW!*

2:59.

Maddie leaped over the final step and ran right into the crown room. It was as high as they could go. Lexi ran in just behind her, fists up, ready to take on the mysterious kidnappers. Caleb was close behind.

The space in the crown was tight enough that it took only a moment to register that their families weren't there. Instead, there was one figure silhouetted against a window in Lady Liberty's crown.

The figure turned. It was Zander Lyon.

CHAPTER 17

Sub divo

Under the wide-open sky

"Congratulations!" he boomed, smiling broadly. An all-white Illuminati-issued tracksuit covered his athletic frame.

Maddie's head was spinning. What was Zander Lyon doing here? Where were Jay and Jessica?

"What the heck, man? I mean, Mr. Lyon, sir?" Lexi exclaimed. "Where are our families?"

Zander pointed toward the window. "Down there," he said. "And safe," he added, looking at Caleb's panicked expression. "See, they're having a blast!"

"What? So they're all okay?" Caleb said in disbelief.

Zander nodded. "Yep!"

Maddie looked below and spotted her and her friends' "kidnapped" families relaxing near the statue's base. "How did you get our families here?" Maddie asked.

"We invited them to a little soiree thrown by LyonCorp," Zander said, "to celebrate your achievements at Camp Minerva this summer. And your success on this final test— you've all passed!"

Maddie could feel her brain trying to catch up, racing from the fear that had coursed through her moments ago to the happy, carefree scene at the party below.

"This whole thing was just a test?" asked Lexi, her eyes wide.

"Yep," answered Zander. "Sorry we had to test you with the whole 'Your loved ones are in mortal danger' thing, but part of being an agent is thinking clearly even when everything important to you is on the line. And you did. Not everyone was able to." He shook his head in disappointment. "But you three . . . what you did was remarkable. You three are special. I'm impressed—and I don't get impressed easily. I once saw a lion, a real lion, play Mozart on the piano, and even that didn't impress me. But you three, you impressed me."

Maddie sighed with relief. This had all been a test. And she had passed. She had passed! And more importantly, Jay and Jessica were safe.

"When can we get started doing real Illuminati missions?" Maddie asked.

"Soon," Zander promised. "But there's another reason I brought you up here."

He pulled Maddie's Electrical Enhancer from his shirt pocket. Well, not the exact one Maddie had made. She could tell immediately this was a better version. Like the one she'd envisioned in her prototype. "To commemorate your induction into the Illuminati's ranks, I'm installing this *new and improved* Electrical Enhancer onto the torch."

"Whoa," Maddie whispered.

"We're pairing Maddie's device with an organic LED bulb—of my own design, of course—so that Lady Liberty's torch can stay lit for the next, oh, eternity," said Zander.

Maddie was not listening. All she could focus on was the Electrical Enhancer—*her* Electrical Enhancer—in Zander Lyon's hands.

He flipped it over carefully, removed a back panel, and held out the device toward Maddie. "I actually need your help, Maddie. I've mastered many technological devices, but I couldn't figure this part out," he said, pointing into the circuit board.

Maddie spotted the mistake immediately. She turned the device off, disconnected and reconnected several wires, and handed it back to Zander. It took her less than a minute.

"Like I said before—mind-blowing," Zander said, nodding approvingly at the device in his outstretched palm. Maddie beamed with pride. Zander removed a small swarm of bee-sized nanodrones from his pants pockets. The buzzing robots plucked the device from his hand and flew out of a crown window to attach it to the torch.

"The Illuminati's mission is to let the light always show the way," Zander said. "And what better way to do that than to use *your invention* to keep Lady Liberty's torch aflame?"

"But won't it take energy from all around it to work? Isn't that stealing?" Maddie asked, remembering what Archibald Archibald had said to her at the engineering competition.

"Borrowing," Zander said, with a wink. Maddie grinned.

"Thanks to your invention," he said, "the Statue of Liberty's torch will be lit forever."

Maddie, Lexi, and Caleb took another look out the window down onto Liberty Island, where strands of twinkling lights now illuminated the party below.

"Can we go down and see our families?" asked Maddie.

"Of course!" Zander said.

The three recruits beamed.

They returned to the base of the Statue of Liberty, and Maddie practically sprinted to Jay and Jessica, who were standing in line for cotton candy next to a Ferris wheel. They were standing with their backs facing her, but she just couldn't wait. She jumped onto Jay's back and gave him a big bear hug.

"Whoa-ho-ho!" said Jay as he turned around, trying to

see her. Maddie released him from her bear hug and giggled. "If it isn't our little genius."

"Maddie!" Jessica screamed. "You're here!"

Maddie grinned and hugged Jessica. "I missed you guys so much! But I'm having so much fun trai—I mean, at camp."

"Yes, indeed she is," said a voice behind her. Maddie, Jessica, and Jay all turned to see Zander Lyon approaching them. His white tracksuit practically glowed in the sunlight. "Maddie is particularly talented. It's almost like she's on a different wavelength from the other kids."

"That's what I always say!" Jessica exclaimed, pulling Maddie close and kissing the top of her head. Maddie looked to her left and saw Caleb and Lexi chatting with their relatives. Well, Lexi and her brothers weren't really chatting. Wrestling was more like it. Caleb caught Maddie's gaze and waved. Auntie Rebecca, a wrinkly old woman in a pink sweater, turned and gave Maddie a nodding smile.

"Dude, thank you so much for the microwaves," Jay said, his eyes the size of golf balls. He was totally starstruck.

"My pleasure! And now, meeting you, I can see where Maddie gets her inquisitive mind from," Zander said, his mischievous-billionaire smile returning.

Jay pointed to himself. "I can't take all the credit," he said, not sensing Zander's sarcasm.

"Well, I hate to break up the party, but our chariot awaits," Zander said, and pulled out his car keys. "Maddie, meet me on the other side of the island in five."

Maddie nodded and turned back toward her cousins.

"I'm so glad you're having a good summer, sweetie," said Jessica, as she gave her another hug. "I love you."

"Yeah, kiddo," said Jay, ruffling her hair. "Tell Zander, maybe next time he could send some new toasters."

Maddie giggled and blew them both kisses. "You got it, Microwave Man!"

CHAPTER 18

Etiam capillus unus habet umbram.

Even one hair casts a shadow.

When they'd all said goodbye to their families, Maddie, Lexi, and Caleb met Zander on the far side of the island, away from the party. He clicked something twice, and a pale blue minivan appeared out of thin air. They all climbed in and soared up and over the Statue of Liberty, circling the seven points on her crown before zooming over the Hudson River. The river sparkled beneath them as they flew toward lower Manhattan. The tall glass Freedom Tower shone like a prism in the sun.

"So the flying cars are . . . legal?" Maddie asked as the car rose, helicopter-style, even higher into the air.

"I don't think so," Zander said. "But remember, I've put

up the cloaking shields. And the Illuminati have a good relationship with the 'official' authorities that goes back decades. We also have agents high up in almost every industry."

The flying car looped and banked with the air currents as they traveled over the Financial District, over the bustling shops of Chinatown and the West Village, and up over Union Square.

They swerved past the stately Flatiron Building, its unique triangular shape like the prow of a ship pointed up Fifth Avenue and Broadway. And then they pulled up next to the tallest building around. It was silver and rectangular, with a pyramidal roof ending in a tall spire.

"May I present the Empire State Building!" Zander said. The car rotated upward ninety degrees and began to fly parallel to the outer walls of the building, like it was zooming up the side.

"Ummm, did I mention I get carsick?" Caleb asked. But the kids couldn't stop smiling. This was more fun than a roller coaster.

"The hundredth floor is ours," Zander said. "Well, technically, we control more of the building than that, but this is our New York satellite office. Are you ready to see it?"

"Uh." Caleb cleared his throat tentatively. "How do we get in? We're up pretty high. Is there a bridge or something?"

"I used to take trapeze classes," Lexi offered. "I could

swing us in one at a time."

Zander chuckled. "As always, I'm impressed by your determination. But it's actually quite simple." He grabbed a rectangular piece of white plastic with a round white button off the dashboard. "Garage door opener. Archibald Archibald bought it at Home Depot."

A section of the Empire State Building's wall of steel and windows started rolling upward, just like a garage door! The car turned horizontal again and parked itself inside.

"See? Simple," Zander repeated. "No need to take the elevator, and we don't have to move the car for street cleanings."

An unfamiliar man stood at the corner of the garage. "Archibald Archibald?" Maddie asked.

He stifled a gasp. "You recognized me?" he asked.

"Nope!" said Maddie. "That's how I knew it was you!"

Archibald smiled. "Right this way," he said with a sweep of his arm.

Archibald Archibald led them through a labyrinth of hallways lit by flaming torches, which cast dramatic shadows over the beige walls and beige-carpeted floors. Except for the flickering torches, it looked like a regular office building on the inside. An emergency exit door swung open just ahead of them, and Killian and Sefu entered, led by another Illuminati official who looked to be high-ranking and important. Killian was complaining loudly, waving his arms. "I just don't understand—we're to be dressed in athletic wear for this event? This just isn't done." He smoothed his pompadour, leaning closer to the official. "My brother is in a secret society at Cambridge, and they get *special robes* just for eating dinner together! And they have to wear silk ties with their crest on them. Why is nobody in this organization wearing ties?"

"I hate wearing ties," Zander whispered. "That's why." Maddie, Lexi, and Caleb giggled the rest of the way down the hall, until a huge set of heavy oak double doors swept open.

As they entered, hundreds of torches flickered light and then shadows across the room. Maddie saw symbols everywhere: on the floor, on the walls, even on holograms floating throughout the space. At the far end of the room, there was a door embossed with a large golden triangle topped by the All-Seeing Eye. It was guarded by a hooded figure.

"Recruits," Volkov said, stepping forward, removing her hood. "Once you step through this door you will have one final chance to leave this world behind. Should you choose to leave, we will wipe your memory and you will go back to the world you used to know. Should you stay, you will no longer be in training. For the rest of your life, you will be subject to the rules that govern every member of this organization. You will be Illuminati super spies."

"It's time," Zander announced. "All recruits, please enter." Volkov opened the door, but Maddie couldn't see inside. She felt a tap on her shoulder and turned to see Sefu smiling at her.

"I'm glad to see you three," he said.

"What about Rolly?" Maddie asked. "Was he in your group for the final test?"

Sefu nodded sadly. "Yeah, he and Killian," he said. But Sefu didn't say anything else. He didn't have to. Whatever happened to Rolly meant that he would no longer become an Illuminati agent. Maddie wondered if Killian had something to do with it.

They shuffled into the room, and Maddie was immediately confused. It was empty, except for three long tables arranged in a semicircle. On the tables were placards, each with a recruit's name on it. Maddie walked up to the placard with her name and found a piece of paper placed next to it.

I, <u>MADDIE ROBINSON</u>, do here hereby pledge to uphold the solemn oath and principles of the Illuminati. By signing this document, I promise to always:

1. *Obey all orders from ranking Illuminati leadership.*
2. *Keep the Illuminati's secrets from all friends, family, and foes.*
3. *Let the light show the way.*
   Signed,

_____

Maddie considered the document and then looked back at the table. Next to her placard was a pen and a little red button that she hadn't noticed before. It said *Do Not Sign*. She wondered what would happen if she pushed it, but she didn't have to wonder for long.

A recruit standing next to her pushed his little red button, and a very pleasant chime began dinging. It got faster and faster until a trapdoor opened underneath him. He was whisked away, through a human-sized vacuum tube, without another word.

But then Maddie thought about her parents. If only they could see how much she had learned, how much she had grown, how much more confidence she had in herself! She felt like she was starting to live up to the legacies of knowledge and exploration they had left for her. Maybe one day her Illuminati skills and connections could even help her discover what had really happened to them.

Sure, this meant that her life would never be normal—and she could never *ever* tell Jay and Jessica. That secret would be hard to keep. But she couldn't imagine going back to the way things had been before. Being in the Illuminati gave her life meaning. And it gave her the chance to be great. Zander Lyon already believed in her enough to install her Electrical Enhancer into the torch of the Statue of Freaking Liberty. That was reason enough.

Maddie picked up the pen and scrawled her signature

at the bottom in her best, most flourishing cursive, almost bursting with pride. She stood tall and looked around at all the other kids. They all looked proud of themselves, too. Suddenly, the walls surrounding the room simply disappeared. Now they were standing in the middle of a huge banquet room, surrounded by people of all ages in golden robes, who cheered when they appeared.

The room was decorated with flowing banners printed with various Illuminati symbols, and the smells of incense, and delicious appetizers, wafted through the air. In the center of the room, on a small dais, stood a golden pyramid that was as tall as Maddie, surrounded by candles. At the top of the triangle was a carving of an eye that seemed to look at Maddie no matter where she stood. Caleb and Lexi walked up to Maddie, and the three joined hands and exchanged smiles.

Volkov and Zander Lyon stood on either side of the pyramid.

Zander raised a glass with a fizzy beverage. "The light will always show the way. Welcome to the Illuminati, super spies."

CHAPTER 19

Per angusta ad augusta
Through difficulty to honor

Maddie wandered around the room, sampling the appetizers. She talked and mingled with the other kids, but there were so many people that after a while she felt a little overwhelmed. She found set of French doors that led out to a terrace. From this high up, she could see the sun setting to the west of Manhattan. The city glittered beneath her and looked almost peaceful, despite the honking car horns and sirens that she could hear, even from a hundred floors up.

As Maddie turned south to see if she could spot the Statue of Liberty from here, the temperature started to drop. She shivered as a damp mist descended over Manhattan, making it hard to see far in the distance. To her right, the sky was crystal clear, a deep violet-blue, dotted with pinpricks of early stars. But as she peered southward, over toward the Statue of Liberty, the sky looked murky and grayish.

"Huh," Lexi said as she and Caleb joined Maddie outside. Lexi pointed out toward the bay. "I can't tell if those are rain clouds or just fog. Doesn't look like what you'd normally expect in this weather."

"What do you mean?" Maddie said.

"It's not unheard of for a coastal mist to gather under these weather conditions," Caleb said. "The humidity would allow for it. It's moving fast, which means there's probably a storm off the coast."

"I guess," Lexi said, frowning slightly.

Even the lights of the buildings much closer to Maddie became rather fuzzy in the mist. The smell of food wafted outside—she inhaled deeply and caught the scents of roast chicken, and cotton candy, and yes, even cheesesteaks.

Maddie stifled a yawn. "Sorry," she said. "Not that discussing the fog isn't interesting. I'm just tired. It's been a long day. But we did it."

As the three went back inside, Volkov clinked a glass to get the room's attention. "Please have a seat with your training groups. Enjoy this dinner celebration," she announced in the same stern tone she used when she was ordering them to do sit-ups.

The buffet included all the favorite foods the agents

had encountered that first day at Camp Minerva. Maddie looked over at Killian, who scowled at anyone else eating tuna tartare, as if they didn't possess sufficiently advanced taste buds to enjoy the uncooked fish as much as he did.

"Do you know what your assignment is yet?" Sefu asked when he sat down next to Maddie. "Mine is Illuminati Control."

"No, I haven't heard anything," she said.

"Mine is European headquarters," Killian boasted. "Too bad for you that the assignments are based on where we all live. I imagine it's hard for those with . . . less desirable origins."

"You scoundrel!" As soon as Maddie heard Lexi's voice, she knew Lexi was balling up her fist. Maddie didn't even have to look.

"It's okay, Lexi," Maddie said quickly. "We don't need his approval. Not after what Zander said about us." She couldn't help but give Killian a smug smile. "We've already made an important contribution. Zander is using *my* Electrical Enhancer to light the torch in the Statue of Lib—"

Volkov, who Maddie didn't even know was within earshot, cut her off abruptly. "Agent," Volkov said, her tone sharp-edged, "we do not *boast* about individual accomplishments. We speak only of the work of the organization."

Killian snickered.

"That said," Volkov added, "all agents should aim to

contribute *something*." She looked pointedly at Killian, who reddened.

After that delightful little speech from Volkov, the new agents finished their meals in near silence. "What do you think our first mission will be?" Maddie whispered to Lexi.

"Hmm." Lexi crunched on a cucumber. "I hope we get to take on cucumber poachers."

"Is there even such a thing?" Maddie asked.

Lexi thought for a second. "Well, there won't be after we get done with them."

A short while later, Volkov reappeared at the front of the room and addressed the new agents. "You will be staying here tonight, and until you return to your home assignments," she said. "I trust you will find the accommodations quite comfortable."

"Better than a hard bench in the middle of Times Square," Lexi muttered.

Volkov fixed their table with a sharp look from her jeweled eye before continuing.

"All your belongings have been transferred from Camp Minerva to your suites here at New York headquarters."

"A suite, finally," Killian said, sounding pleased.

Before they retired to their suites, Maddie, Lexi, and Caleb each grabbed a glass of punch and stepped outside for a look over the city. The view was amazing—buildings with thousands of windows lit up against the red and white lights of the traffic streaming in a grid far below them. Plus they could see Lady Liberty, her torch lit forever thanks to Maddie's invention.

"Volkov said she didn't want me talking about my device," Maddie said.

"She's probably jealous," Lexi said.

"Or she needs to feel like she's in charge," Caleb offered. "And if you're proving yourself to be important to Zander, maybe she doesn't like it."

"I bet that's exactly what it is," said Maddie. "Volkov may have it out for us, but we're agents now. We proved ourselves." The trio clinked their punch glasses, took a final swig, and then deposited the glasses on a tray before heading toward their accommodations.

Maddie's suite had a living room area with a love seat, an armchair, and an ottoman, all upholstered in tasteful gold and beige tones, with a slight retro look. There was a private bathroom, stocked with strawberry-scented shampoo, chocolate-scented conditioner, vanilla-scented fancy soaps, caramel-scented toothpaste (which was kind of gross, actually), Zander's favorite brand of hair/goatee gel, and a fluffy bathrobe with a discreet golden triangle embroidered on the chest. In the bedroom sat a full-sized (non-bunk, non-magnetized) bed, covered in a dozen pillows.

As Volkov had promised, Maddie's belongings from Camp Minerva were set out on a sleek wooden bureau. Maddie's Snoopy was tucked in among the pillows on the bed. She felt a little embarrassed that someone else must have packed her stuffed animal and put it there.

As Maddie lay in her ultra-comfy bed, using the breathing techniques she'd learned in Meditation Training, she couldn't shake the feeling that something just hadn't seemed right that evening. What was that face Volkov had made when Maddie talked about her Electrical Enhancer? Was there something going on—some problem—that they weren't telling the kids about? Did it have to do with the mysterious Obscuritas? Maddie felt like it was just outside her reach, the way her Electrical Enhancer's function had been before she finally nailed the prototype.

Her dad had taught her to think critically—to judge with a clear head—but Maddie wasn't sure where to start. She tried to walk through all the unusual events—but *everything* had been unusual since the Recruiter showed up at her science competition. But Maddie would have to figure it out tomorrow. Her breathing techniques were working. And within a minute of her head hitting the pillow, she was asleep.

CHAPTER 20

In absentia lucis, tenebrae vincunt.
In the absence of light, darkness prevails.

The next morning, Maddie woke early. She had just finished getting dressed and brushing her teeth when she heard a loud knock on her door. She adjusted her hoodie, spat out her toothpaste, and took a moment to remember she was in a fancy Illuminati bedroom a hundred stories up in the Empire State Building.

She padded over to the door and opened it. "Good morning," she said to Lexi.

Lexi bounded straight into the room and started pacing. "I still don't understand the deal with your Electro-majig. It's not dangerous, right? I know I'm not the tech genius, so can you tell me again why it's not dangerous?"

"It's the *amount* of power it requires," Maddie said. "Just a little. It's not dangerous. I promise."

"Okay, good," Lexi exhaled. "Because it's gone."

"Power can't just be *gone*. That's not how energy *works*. It's—"

"No, Maddie," Caleb said from where he'd appeared behind them. "She means *the Statue of Liberty*. *It's gone.* Look." He crossed to the window and threw open the thick curtains. Light streamed into the room. Caleb gestured out the window toward where Maddie's device had lit the torch the evening before.

"What?" Maddie couldn't believe what she was seeing. Or rather, what she wasn't seeing. There was no torch, no crown, no statue . . . just an expanse of grayish-blue river water. Caleb handed her a pair of high-tech binoculars. She aimed them to where Lady Liberty had proudly stood just last night . . . and saw only a large concrete base, holding up exactly nothing.

Before Maddie could process this news, a figure appeared at the door. He knocked politely, even though the door was already open.

"Who are you?" Lexi asked.

"Archibald Archibald? Or at least, I think so?" Maddie asked. She couldn't be totally sure.

"You've seen," he said, gesturing toward the window. Maddie looked through the binoculars again to where the Statue of Liberty used to be. Now the place was swarming with cops, waving tourists aside and unrolling reams of yellow crime-scene tape.

"Zander needs to see you three in his office," Archibald said, his voice low and urgent.

Maddie nodded. Her heart was beating wildly as they followed Archibald Archibald through what seemed like miles of beige hallways to an unmarked door. The Recruiter opened the door barely more than a foot and pushed the three agents inside.

"How does something that big just disappear?" Zander muttered, pacing around his office. The room was decorated in a bold 1920s style, with leather seats and gold accents. On a shelf, next to a golden owl statuette, was an old-fashioned radio with rounded edges, making it look like a locomotive hurtling forward. Everything was shiny and subtly luxurious, like Zander's curved desk, which appeared to be formed out of a single giant piece of wood.

Zander looked stressed. He had dark shadows under his eyes, and his goatee, which was usually coifed to perfection, was pointing every which way. "We've got our people searching for clues all over. Anything related to the Statue of Liberty. We've got agents down by Liberty Island, combing the area for any hint of who did this."

"We want to help!" said Maddie without hesitation.

"First I need to know what you three know," he went on. "Did you see anything—or anyone—other than us at the Statue of Liberty yesterday? Did you tell *anyone* about the

Electrical Enhancer . . . even anybody here? Has anyone from Obscuritas tried to contact you?"

Maddie opened her mouth to respond, but Lexi leaped in. "No one's tried to contact me," she said.

"Or me," said Maddie.

"Me neither," said Caleb.

Zander sat at a huge desk and peered into his S.M.A.R.T.W.A.T.C.H.'s display, absently stroking his disheveled goatee.

"I wouldn't want the Electrical Enhancer to fall into the wrong hands," Maddie admitted.

"Excuse me, what's Obscuritas?" Caleb blurted.

Zander looked dazed. He frowned at his display, and then he tapped on the holographic keyboard. "Oh no," he said. "The Statue of Liberty has been stolen!"

Maddie was unnerved. "Uh, we know that already," she said. "That's what this meeting is about."

"No, a *miniature* Statue of Liberty was also stolen from the Smithsonian American Art Museum in Washington, DC," Zander said, sending a hologram to the center of the room. The 3D image showed a museum room with an empty pedestal. Zander tapped a few more keys and the scene changed. "This is what it usually looks like." In the image, there was a replica of the Statue of Liberty rendered in dark brown metal perched on the pedestal, and it looked to be about four feet tall.

"Why would someone steal a tiny model of the Statue

of Liberty if they've already stolen the real thing?" asked Caleb.

Zander turned to the three agents. "You asked about Obscuritas," he said, his expression darkening. Even though they were in a secure room, he looked around and lowered his voice. "Our intelligence team suspects that Obscuritas is behind this thievery . . . as well as Lady Liberty's disappearance. The most likely hypothesis is that the two thefts are related. If we find the tiny one, it might help us locate the big one."

Maddie's heart beat a little faster. "It has finally happened. Obscuritas has made its move," Zander whispered.

"But what *is* Obscuritas?" Lexi asked.

Zander shook his head sadly. "It's a Latin word meaning 'darkness' or 'obscurity.' As in, the *opposite* of the Illuminati."

Caleb nodded. "Makes sense."

"No, it does *not* make sense, because why would anyone want to be the *opposite* of an illustrious and lofty world-saving organization like the Illuminati?" Zander was shouting now. "Sorry, I didn't mean to yell at you there. I've just been dealing with this problem for a very long time."

He took a deep breath. When he continued speaking, his voice was so somber that Maddie's pulse quickened. "Obscuritas is a shadowy organization of former Illuminati agents who have very different goals for the world. They're trying to erase Lady Liberty and her light—aka, everything that the Illuminati stand for—from existence!"

Maddie thought back to upgrading the statue with her Electrical Enhancer, just yesterday. And now someone had dared to steal it? "We're in. How we can help?" she said confidently.

"I am going to send the three of you on a mission to recover the statue. You're new, but you're the agents I trust the most. But be careful. Obscuritas spies could be anywhere, pretending to be anyone. I don't want to scare you, but their leader is a terrifying mastermind who will stop at nothing to control the entire world. His name is . . . *Doug*."

"What kind of evil mastermind name is Doug?" Caleb asked.

"I hope you are ready for your first real mission," said Zander. "Head to the Smithsonian Institution in DC and locate the missing model of Lady Liberty. It's not much to go on, but right now, it's the only lead we've got."

CHAPTER 21

De omnibus dubitandum.

Be suspicious of everything.

The kids quickly got dressed in new civilian camouflage gear. These were patterned to look like their normal everyday clothes—a hoodie for Maddie, an oversized jacket with suede elbow patches for Caleb, and overalls for Lexi—but were actually made out of the same high-tech fabrics as their camp gear. They'd be able to blend into the touristy crowd at the Smithsonian American Art Museum and still run, jump, fight, or explore . . . whatever the situation called for.

Zander stuffed some cash into a fanny pack. "This is all I can give you," he said. "But this is a version of my own personal go bag. It's got tools, everything you need to track down the mini Statue of Liberty. And gum. Quick Zanec-dote for ya: you never know when you'll need gum."

"Isn't that just a saying?" Maddie mumbled as he handed the bag to her.

"Take this, too," he said, handing her a small electronic device shaped like an elongated clamshell with an antenna.

"What *is* that?" Lexi asked, peering at the device.

"Wow," Caleb marveled. "It's an early cell phone. I've never seen one in person."

"Is this from the Smithsonian, too?" Lexi asked, extending the antenna, then sliding it back down, with a look of wonder on her face.

"In addition to super high tech, we also use older technology, so we're less easily hacked," Zander explained. "Contact me with what you find. I'm the first number on speed dial."

"Got it," Maddie said. Jay and Jessica had each had phones like this until a few years ago. "So I guess we'll head to the train station, then."

"Good luck, agents." Zander's eyes were already back on his S.M.A.R.T.W.A.T.C.H. display.

Archibald Archibald, appearing from out of nowhere, opened the door for them to depart.

"How do we, uh, leave?" Lexi asked him.

"I'll walk you," Archibald said with an encouraging smile. "We'll just go down this—"

"That won't be necessary," Volkov said briskly, also

appearing out of nowhere. "You're needed here. I will personally escort our newest, least experienced, and therefore least capable agents outside," she said.

Maddie bristled at Volkov's words. Why did she hate them so much? Did she blame Maddie for what had happened, since it was *her* invention that had been stolen? Maddie wasn't the one popping out of tree trunks, sending whispered messages. After all, Volkov had known this was coming. If she was going to blame anyone, it should be herself.

Volkov led them down a maze of hallways, turning right and left so many times past so many identical doors set into identical beige walls that Maddie felt like they were walking in circles. She led them into an elevator. "I will take you to the front of the building. I trust that you can find your way to your destination in Washington, DC, from there," she said.

"Um, sure," Maddie lied. Did she know off the top of her head how to get from New York City to DC? No. But was she going to ask Volkov? Absolutely not.

When they emerged from the elevator, Maddie stopped to re-Velcro her shoe, which had gotten loose somehow. "Sorry, sorry, sorry," she murmured. As she bent down, the ancient cell phone slid out of the pocket of her hoodie and hit the floor with a tinny clunk. *Great, I already broke it,* Maddie thought. This mission was already off to a not-so-great start.

Volkov bent down to help Maddie. "You dropped this," said the Eastern European agent, handing Maddie the phone and a black hunk of plastic that Maddie didn't recognize. "I don't expect to hear from you again until your mission is complete."

"This isn't mine—" Maddie started to say as they reached the exit, but Volkov was already gone in a whirl of her fitted black trench coat, and the three agents were outside on the New York City sidewalk, totally alone.

"Okay, so now what?" Lexi asked, looking around.

They huddled under an awning to avoid the stifling August heat while they figured out their next step. "To the train station!" said Caleb. "Which is . . . this way?" he said, pointing east.

"When we were flying above the city, I'm pretty sure I saw the train station over this way," said Lexi, pointing her thumb west.

Maddie pulled the black piece of plastic from her fanny pack. She'd seen Archibald Archibald and Zander use a similar device to unlock the minivans. *It's her car key!*

"I think Volkov just dropped the key to her flying car. We should give it back, right?" asked Maddie, more to herself. "Right?"

"Though she did say she didn't want to see us again . . . ," said Lexi.

She looked at Caleb, who finally spoke. "We *could* return the keys. Or we could . . . ?"

Lexi finished his thought. "Borrow her car?"

"Just for the day, of course!" said Maddie.

"Just for the day!" agreed Lexi.

"And we'll return it in perfect condition," said Caleb.

"Perfect condition!" agreed Maddie. "She won't even know it's gone!"

Maddie squeezed the button. *Beep, BEEP, beeeep,* a familiar car horn sounded nearby.

"There!" Lexi said, pointing to a minivan on the opposite side of the street. This one was maroon in color but had a white replacement door on the passenger side and a faded golden triangle ornament on the hood.

"This is the ugliest vehicle I have ever seen," said Caleb.

"That just means the inside will be even cooler!" said Lexi. They ran over and jumped into the van.

Before they took off, Maddie dumped out the contents of the fanny pack onto the van's center console to take stock of all her new gear. Among the expected tools was a folded piece of paper. Maddie opened it. "It's a handwritten note from Zander," she said.

"Read it!" said Lexi.

"'Agents: Trust each other. Trust your instincts. You can do this.'"

"Sounds like a plan," Lexi said approvingly. "Let's go." She reached for her seat belt, and Maddie scooped the items back into the fanny pack and clipped it around her waist. She checked to make sure her tricked-out phone was in her pants pocket. *I'd better keep these tools handy,* she thought. *We have no idea what we're going to need on this mission.*

"To Washington!" Maddie called to the car's supercomputer brain.

"WOO-HOO!" Lexi exclaimed. "We're off!!"

They waited, but the car didn't move.

"Please provide more information," a digitized voice announced.

"Oh, right," said Maddie sheepishly. "Take us to Washington, *DC*, please . . . Smithsonian American Art Museum. Thank you."

The car took off. Maddie settled into her seat as they zoomed over Bryant Park and the New York Public Library, with the stone lions out front. They climbed, higher, higher into the sky. "I've always said, the only way to see New York City is from the air," said Caleb.

"You've *always* said that?" said Lexi teasingly.

"Well . . . I'm going to start saying it," he said with a laugh.

Several police sirens started blaring. "Activate the cloaking shields?" Maddie called tentatively. She had no idea if those sirens were because of them, but she sure wasn't going to wait around to find out.

CHAPTER 22

Excelsior!
Onward and upward!

In the flying minivan, the kids zoomed over the skyscrapers of Manhattan, then over the sparkling Hudson River, busy with tour boats and ferries and barges. They flew over bridges and passed a flock of geese, traveling in a V formation. Maddie noticed a button with the outline of a goose on it on the car ceiling.

"What does that do?" Caleb asked.

Maddie pressed the button. A loud *HONK* burst out from the car, and the geese honked back. "I think it's just a way to say hello to geese," she said, impressed by the Illuminati's thoughtfulness.

Their car passed over suburbs and little towns, connected

by a web of train tracks and highways. They soared over brown and yellow fields, and over the tops of deep green, leafy forests.

Lexi fiddled with the built-in mini-fridge, pouring jets of sparkling water into little biodegradable cups. "They have cucumber flavor!" She grinned.

Caleb stared at the car's interior, taking note of all the features. "What's this do?" he asked, flicking a metal toggle. "Masssssaaaaage chaaaaaaairs," he said as their seats vibrated powerfully. He shuddered and flicked it off. "So, how does this thing fly?" he asked Maddie. "Do you think it has some sort of antigravity tech?"

Maddie made a disappointed face. "I wish I knew! I'd love to take this apart and learn how it works." She leaned back in her seat and watched the world speed by. She noticed the view was filling up with buildings and huge, circular highways.

"Is this DC already?" asked Lexi.

"No, it can't be," Caleb said. But as he looked out below, the Capitol and the Washington Monument came into view.

"Whoa," Lexi said.

Maddie couldn't believe the speed of their trip. *It's going to be hard going back to hour-and-a-half bus rides after this,* she thought.

The flying car descended gently over a neighborhood with brick town houses and tree-lined streets. It landed in an alleyway and found a space to park behind an overflowing dumpster. The young agents turned onto 8th Street.

"We're here," said Maddie.

"Whoa! This place looks like something from ancient Rome or Greece," Lexi said, pointing to the Smithsonian American Art Museum. Tired vacationers leaned against the building to try to escape the morning heat. The city was bustling, but the line to get into the museum moved quickly.

"This building houses the National Portrait Gallery, too," said Caleb.

"How many of the famous people in there are actually Illuminati members?" Maddie asked.

"Like, all of them!" answered Lexi. "Probably," she added. "So what's the plan?"

"Let's go in and find out where they kept the model Statue of Liberty," Maddie said.

They climbed up the stone steps and entered the museum, which, thankfully, was free to the public. Inside the building, the kids paused to stare. Golden sunlight poured from large square windows into a grand atrium several stories high, filled with graceful columns, an elegant black-and-white marble floor, and giant round chandeliers. Tour groups and families filled the lobby, clutching maps and taking selfies.

Maddie, Caleb, and Lexi followed the crowd into an interior courtyard—so huge that there were even trees inside it—lining a central strip inlaid with gleaming rectangular reflecting pools. Maddie craned her neck to admire the ceiling, a futuristic webbing of white beams and glass, creating the biggest skylight she'd ever seen. Caleb grabbed a museum map from a holder near the door and consulted it. "We want to go to the South Wing, second floor," he said.

The kids backtracked to the lobby and climbed a sweeping, semicircular stairway to the second floor. They wove through clumps of people, ignoring the paintings and statues on display.

"We should come back here sometime," said Lexi. "You know, when we're not on duty."

"Definitely," said Maddie.

"We might be better off studying at Camp Minerva," said Caleb. "If we want to learn the *real* history."

They followed signs for *The Industrial Era*, but as they approached, they saw a dark gray floor-to-ceiling panel blocking off the entrance to the exhibit hall. Maddie and Caleb instinctively slowed at the sight of the panel, but Lexi barreled ahead, as if she were going to bust right on through.

Maddie and Caleb hustled to catch up and noticed a small plaque that read *Please Excuse This Inconvenience.— Museum Management.*

"I guess we should have expected this," said Maddie.

"I don't see a door." Lexi frowned. "I mean, I could

break through it, but it would cause a stir."

Before Maddie could advise against breaking anything or causing a ruckus in one of the nation's most important museums, a tall man in a navy-blue uniform stepped briskly in front of them, startling Lexi into backing up a few steps. "Unfortunately, this area is not open to the public right now," he informed them in a deep, slow voice. "For the . . . foreseeable . . . future," he said, before walking away.

"There's got to be another way in," Caleb mused. He tapped his fingers lightly over the museum map as he studied it. "Hmm . . . over here." He pointed to a section of the floor plan. "See this? There's space between the exhibit area and the public stairwell."

"But what does that mean?" Maddie asked, staring at the map.

"It can't just be empty space," Caleb said. "There's probably a second stairwell for employees and volunteers. If so, it might have access directly to the exhibit halls."

"Well, let's go!" Lexi exclaimed.

"But . . . let's try to act like regular tourists, not like we're on a top secret mission," Maddie whispered, and Caleb nodded vigorously in agreement. "We don't want to draw any attention to ourselves."

They walked toward the spot Caleb had identified on the map, then up to the third floor, where they figured it would be less crowded, and well out of sight of the plodding security guard who'd spoken to them.

Near the third-floor stairwell, as Caleb had predicted, there was an unmarked door. It was locked, of course.

"Cover me," Maddie said. "I can get us in."

She pulled out a tube of clear plastic from her fanny pack. It was one of the tools she'd used at Camp Minerva's lab; something that looked like nothing special on the outside but was actually quite useful.

"It's a tube of flexible smart-plastic particles," Maddie explained. "They'll intelligently adjust to any space they're inserted into. Perfect for making keys." She pushed it into the lock. "One . . . two . . . three . . ." She turned the key counterclockwise. *CLICK!* "We're in," said Maddie, grinning and stepping into a second stairwell.

Lexi and Caleb followed. They descended two flights of steps and then cautiously opened the door at the bottom.

What struck Maddie first was how *normal* everything looked. Lexi seemed similarly confused. "Where's all the yellow crime-scene tape and security guards?" she asked. "I don't see a single thing out of place!"

Then Maddie saw it—in the middle of the room was a pedestal. And it was empty.

"There it . . . isn't," she murmured. She took a few photos with the phone she'd built at Camp Minerva, then switched the phone's camera to a modded hyper-zoom mode to look for footprints. Nothing. Then something near the pedestal—something gleaming—caught her eye.

She walked closer. A nickel was on the ground. She reached

down to pick it up, but it wouldn't budge. *That's weird.* About a foot away, she noticed another one. She walked over and tried to pick it up, but it wouldn't budge, either.

She scanned the room, noting even more nickels. There were eight in total, each one tails-side up. And they formed a perfect octagon. *What the heck?*

"Hey, Caleb, get a look at this," Maddie said.

Caleb jogged over. "Eight nickels. All tails-side up . . . and in an octagon shape . . ." His eyes lit up.

"On the tails side of the nickel is Thomas Jefferson's house, Monticello. I read a biography of it," he began.

"You read a biography of a house?" asked Lexi.

Caleb ignored her and continued. "Thomas Jefferson

built the house to his exact specifications. The domed rotunda room at Monticello has *eight* sides. Jefferson believed that the octagon shape would lead him to enlightenment."

"Enlightenment?" Maddie asked. "Like the Illuminati?" *Was Thomas Jefferson an Illuminati member?* "Maybe his house—"

"Monticello," said Caleb.

"Maybe Monticello has a clue for us?" Maddie asked her friends.

"Seems obvious to me!" said Lexi. "Whoever stole the mini Statue of Liberty wants us to go to Thomas Jefferson's house, in . . . ?"

"In Virginia," said Caleb.

Maddie wasn't sure that it *was* obvious. In fact, it wasn't much to go on at all. But it was all they had. "Okay, let's go!" she said.

They hurried past the slow-talking security guard (Lexi stuck out her tongue at him behind his back) and out the front door. They ran back to the minivan.

"To Monticello—in Charlottesville, Virginia," Maddie instructed the flying vehicle. With a gentle revving of the engine and an upward lurch, they rose into the air and were off!

CHAPTER 23

Si monumentum equires
If you seek his monument

They flew over green fields, highways, and towns, until the minivan touched down on a rural Virginia road about twenty miles from Jefferson's home. Then it auto-drove the rest of the way, pulling smoothly into a parking spot near the Monticello Visitor Center, a sleek wooden building that looked sort of old and sort of modern at the same time.

Maddie instantly recognized the main house from the back of the nickel. It was a stately redbrick mansion with a large white dome and four grandiose stone columns in the front.

Despite a breeze through the trees, the late summer heat was sticky and thick. Groups of sweaty kids stood clustered around in front of the Visitor Center. In most groups, the kids and their chaperones all had matching, brightly colored shirts.

"We need to sneak in with a group," Lexi said. "But that's going to be tough, since they're all dressed alike."

"There's got to be a group we can blend in with," said Caleb, looking around.

"There?" Lexi asked, pointing to kids gathered under the shade of a large tree. "They look like they're our age and aren't wearing matching shirts."

Caleb shook his head. "Not that group. Look at the adults, classic type A authority figures. They have clipboards, and they're actively watching the kids. They'll notice us fast."

"What about over there?" Maddie asked, shielding her eyes with one hand and gesturing with the other to a stretch of pavement where a group of kids were acting like they had never been in public before—jumping on each other, pretend-fighting, yelling, and smacking each other with their backpacks. Maddie could practically hear the lecture her teacher would have given her class about "embarrassing our school" if they had acted like this on a field trip.

Maddie spotted a solitary, flustered-looking adult among the rowdy students. He appeared to be asking them to line up, but so far only two kids had complied. The teacher looked nervous and totally unable to corral his students. "That's a summer school class—with a substitute teacher," Maddie said with a grin. "Perfect."

The trio followed the unruly class through the Visitor Center, then squeezed onto a tiny shuttle bus that dropped them off at the main building they were there to explore.

Just like at the Smithsonian, the inside of Monticello was crowded with field trippers and tourists from all over the world. "This is amazing," Maddie said, looking around at the mansion.

"The house took Thomas Jefferson forty years to build," said Caleb. "He—ahem, his *slaves, actually*—grew hundreds of types of fruits and vegetables here. He even tried to make wine, but that didn't work."

"Even an Illuminati genius can fail sometimes," said Lexi.

Inside the house, people took photos and consulted maps, and little kids hollered for ice cream. The trio wove their way through the crowd to the dome room, which was painted in pale yellow with a white ceiling. "Let's split up to look for clues," Maddie suggested as they entered, "and meet back in a few minutes."

Lexi picked up a paper map a visitor had dropped and then got nose-to-nose with the rotunda walls, searching for any sign of a message. Caleb bent down to inspect the white wooden baseboards, for any hidden panels or other clues.

Maddie walked over to an empty, old wooden bench and sat down, taking it all in. It still seemed impossible that she—Maddie Robinson—and Thomas Jefferson might be connected through the Illuminati. The thought gave her chills.

She let her gaze wander up to the smooth curves of the ceiling and then back down, where reflections from the round windows made circles of light on the wooden floor. Maddie noticed that each bright circle was crisscrossed with identical lines of shadow. She glanced up at a window, confirming that the shadow lines were from strips of wood separating the windowpanes.

Maybe the crisscross pattern means something, she mused. *Like it's a map of streets or trails.* But the bright circle from the dome's skylight was different. Its shadow lines didn't crisscross at all. They just formed a triangle.

A triangle!

Maddie jumped from the bench. She hurried over to the circle of light on the floor and squatted down.

The flooring around the triangle was unremarkable— no messages scratched into the wood, no loose boards that might lift up to reveal a clue. Nothing but light from an old window making a bright patch on an old floor.

The triangle had to mean something, didn't it?

She thought of her cousin Jessica's response every time Maddie came home with whatever made-up award she had received from a competition, while the real winners from fancy schools went home with blue ribbons or trophies. "You're just on a different frequency than those other kids," Jessica would always tell her.

She reached into her pocket and pulled out her modified phone, her eyes landing immediately on the button that read UFL. The ultra-frequency light. Maddie laughed out loud before she could stop herself. *A different frequency.* It was worth a try.

She glanced up to make sure no one was watching, and then she shined the ultra-frequency light on the triangle.

Nothing.

She moved the UFL's beam so it was above the triangle.

43

A number appeared on the floor! She moved the UFL beam to the left and right of the 43.

14

12

114343

This was it.

Maddie stood up. She used the volume buttons on the phone to widen the UFL beam and followed it farther and farther along the floor.

	14	
1		**2**
1 1 4 3 4 3		
9	**17**	**11**
28	**6**	**14**
11	**7**	**90**
3	**2**	**6**
14	**2**	**7**
14	**7**	**2**
42	**3**	**2**
14	**43**	**11**
2	**7**	**5**
11	**14**	**1**
65	**16**	**16**
3	**3**	**11**
42	**1**	**6**
3		**13**

The numbers formed the shape of an obelisk.

Maddie snapped a photo of the numbers, then grabbed Lexi and Caleb. "I found something!" she half whispered, half yelled with excitement. She hustled them over to the bench and explained her discovery. "When viewed with high-frequency light, there are numbers hidden on the floor," she explained breathlessly. "And they form an obelisk!"

"Maybe the numbers are related to another obelisk?" wondered Caleb aloud. "So where are famous obelisks? Remember our Illuminati Architecture lecture?"

"Right!" Maddie said. "There's the Washington Monument. . . . There are some in Egypt. . . ."

She turned to see Lexi holding out the map from the Visitor Center. "And there's one right here," Lexi said, bouncing with excitement as the bench creaked under them. She pointed to the words *Jefferson's Grave* on the Monticello map, where an arrow pointed to a small obelisk.

Fifteen minutes later, they arrived at the obelisk. Caleb and Maddie were out of breath from letting Lexi set the pace to the grave site. It was a small, fenced-in area surrounded by trees, containing a few small grave markers with Jefferson's own six-foot-tall gravestone in the center. Lexi, who hadn't broken a sweat, read aloud the epitaph that was inscribed on the stone:

"HERE WAS BURIED
THOMAS JEFFERSON
AUTHOR OF THE

"The numbers in the rotunda were in the shape of an obelisk," Maddie reminded them.

Caleb ran his fingers through his hair, deep in thought. "Maybe the numbers from the rotunda correspond to the letters on Jefferson's gravestone?"

Maddie nodded. "Yes! So, for instance, the number fourteen, at the very top of the obelisk, is the first letter of a hidden message that someone left for us to find."

"The fourteenth letter is the *T* in Thomas Jefferson," said Lexi. So that's the first letter of the message?" Maddie nodded.

They got into a decoding rhythm. Caleb recited a number, Maddie counted to that letter on the epitaph, and Lexi wrote it down on their map. Another number, another count, another letter recorded.

Minutes later, they huddled around the paper to read the complete message:

**THE ILLUMINATIS' GREATEST SECRET
LIES WITH POOR RICHARD**

"Who's Poor Richard?" Lexi asked.

"It's an old nickname for Benjamin Franklin," Caleb responded. "Where could he be lying?"

"Maybe Ben Franklin is lying in his bed?" offered Lexi.

"If so," said Caleb, "then our next stop must be Ben Franklin's house!"

"Can't be," Maddie said, shaking her head.

"What do you mean?" Lexi asked.

"The house isn't there anymore." She hadn't known the history of Monticello, but she sure knew Philly. "Where the house used to be is now the Benjamin Franklin Museum."

"Well, whatever is located there now, it sure seems like someone is trying to point us in that direction, right?" asked Caleb.

It wasn't much to go on, but they had to try. Maybe there would be another Illuminati manhole cover or an invisible door leading somewhere spectacular. All Maddie hoped was that it would lead them one step closer to finding Obscuritas and recovering the Statues of Liberty.

"Poor Richard is a nickname for *Benjamin Franklin*?" Lexi was saying, her head cocked to one side. "How on earth did they get *Richard* from *Benjamin*? That doesn't make any—"

"We'll look it up on the way," Maddie interrupted. "Right now, we need to fly to Philadelphia!"

CHAPTER 24

Aere perennius
More lasting than bronze

Maddie felt a rush of familiarity as they flew over Philadelphia's Benjamin Franklin Bridge and crossed into the city limits. Even though her apartment with Jay and Jessica was on the outskirts of town, she'd visited Center City countless times between class field trips and science competitions. Even her bus transfer to school required her to walk a few city blocks.

As the car parked itself in a garage, Caleb took off his seat belt. "I'm never going to get tired of having a flying car," he said. "So where to, Maddie?"

Maddie led them around a corner. "This is Benjamin Franklin's house. Or at least, where it used to be."

They used their cash to buy tickets to the Benjamin

Franklin Museum so they could get a good look at the court-yard. It held what the architects called a "ghost house," a reconstruction of where Franklin's house once stood, crafted out of just a few spare steel beams. The courtyard was lined with low trees and had a breezy, parklike atmosphere.

"So, I guess we start looking for something Ben Franklin–like," Maddie said hesitantly. But they couldn't find anything that had to do with Poor Richard's bed or even his bedroom. Maddie tried to look inconspicuous as she checked under a bench for a clue. She pretended to tie her shoelace, even though her shoes had Velcro straps.

Caleb and Lexi couldn't find anything either. "Anyone spot anything . . . clue-like?" Caleb asked.

"I've got nothing," said Lexi. "Just normal museum stuff."

They checked each cobblestone and brick for anything that looked like it might have to do with the Illuminati or Obscuritas, but after a full hour of searching, they recon-vened on a bench outside the museum, dejected.

"You know," Maddie said, "this isn't the only thing in Philadelphia that's dedicated to Benjamin Franklin. There's the bridge we just flew over and a park with his name, and of course, Independence Hall." She continued, looking up local sites on her S.M.A.R.T.W.A.T.C.H., "There's even a Benjamin Franklin dry cleaner's, a Benjamin Franklin watch repair store, a Benjamin Franklin pet store. . . ."

"Benjamin Franklin would probably roll over in his grave if he knew how many people were making money off his name," said Caleb.

And then it clicked. Maddie turned to Lexi and Caleb. Their eyes were also widened with realization. "Poor Richard isn't lying in a bed!" said Maddie.

"He's lying in his grave!" said Lexi.

"Great work, guys," said Caleb.

"He's buried only a block from here! I've been to Franklin's grave site on many school field trips," Maddie said. She led the way, past old monuments and historic meetinghouses still standing in between modern coffee shops and hotels.

When they arrived at Christ Church Burial Ground, it was over a hundred degrees outside, and the sun was beating down on them. Maddie was too excited to care about the fact that she was sweating buckets.

"Hang on!" she exclaimed, running into a drugstore across the street. She came back minutes later holding crayons and notebooks, and the three of them entered the cemetery after paying their one-dollar entrance fee.

"Crayons?" asked Lexi.

Maddie smiled. "Trust me," she said.

A park ranger eyed them warily. "What brings a couple'a kids like yourselves to a cemetery on such a warm summer day? You're not troublemakers, are you?" the sweaty park ranger asked, while holding a motorized handheld fan up to her glistening face.

Maddie, Caleb, and Lexi turned on their most adorable innocent smiles and held up their brand-new box of crayons.

"Summer homework assignment," Maddie said. "Our teacher wants us to bring gravestone rubbings to our first day of history class. We're learning about the Founding Fathers."

The park ranger nodded absently. She'd no doubt heard this hundreds of times before. Nearly every grade in Philadelphia had a unit about the Founding Fathers, since they were so close geographically to where the country began.

"Nice to see young people today taking their education seriously," said the park ranger. "Keep up the good work, young scholars." The ranger walked off, leaving them alone to find Ben Franklin's grave marker.

"Come on. It's over here," said Maddie. She led them to a giant marble slab with Benjamin Franklin's name on it. It was covered in pennies, placed there by visitors.

"What is *this* about?" Lexi asked.

"A penny saved is a penny earned," said Caleb.

"Yes, I know," said Lexi.

"No, *that's* what the pennies are about," said Caleb. "Benjamin Franklin was the person who made that quote famous."

"Ben Franklin said that?" asked Lexi. "I thought my mom came up with it."

Maddie looked at the grave. The marble slab wasn't sticking upright out of the ground like some gravestones. It was lying flat against the ground and was the size of a grown man, almost like a cellar door. "How do we get in?" asked Maddie.

"Beats me," Lexi said. "I've never broken into a grave before." She reached down and tried to lift the slab, but it didn't budge.

"I knew it would be too heavy," Caleb said.

"It's not too heavy," Lexi said, a bit defensively. "It's just sealed very tightly. I can't get a good grip on it."

"Hmm," Maddie said, pulling out her tricked-out phone. None of the upgrades she'd given it seemed right.

"Hmm," Lexi echoed, pawing through the fanny pack that Maddie was wearing. "Maybe there's something in here we can use."

She pulled out a small rectangular object, no bigger than her palm, and began unfolding various gadgets from the main contraption.

"It's like an Illuminati Swiss Army knife," Maddie observed as Lexi unfolded a series of tiny working drills from the credit-card-sized object. "I don't even recognize some of these tools." She wiped the sweat from her forehead. "But we know someone who can help."

"We do?" Lexi asked.

Caleb smiled. "Of course. We can always count on our fellow agents."

With a few taps on her S.M.A.R.T.W.A.T.C.H., Maddie dialed Sefu, at Illuminati HQ in Cairo, for a video call. She could tell that he had been asleep, but he quickly perked up when he realized that his fellow agents needed help.

"Sefu, any idea what these tools are?" Maddie used her phone's camera, and instantly, a hologram of the Illuminati

Swiss Army knife popped up on Sefu's desk projector.

"What are you trying to accomplish?" Sefu asked.

Lexi and Caleb looked at Maddie, who lowered her voice. "We're, uh . . . sort of breaking into Benjamin Franklin's grave," Maddie told him.

"What?" Sefu knocked over a can of cola from his desk in shock.

"If it helps, we think it's not really a grave," said Caleb, "but an Illuminati base. We hope."

Maddie could tell they now had Sefu's interest. "Let me send a satellite to your location," he said. "There's one nearby. I can use the satellite's depth sensor and . . . HUH!" Maddie hoped Sefu's shock meant he had good news for them. "Your suspicions were correct!"

"Yes!" cried Maddie.

"I'm scanning the area now, and you appear to be at the entrance of a small network of underground tunnels." Maddie watched Sefu manipulate the hologram of the Illuminati Swiss Army knife in front of him. "You have here a diamond blade cutter. It should be sharp enough to cut through the stone."

"Thank you, Sefu!" said Lexi into Maddie's S.M.A.R.T.W.A.T.C.H.

"Good luck, agents," said Sefu, signing off.

They set to work. Lexi used the blade cutter to cut through the stone's seal, while Maddie and Caleb pretended to make a rubbing of Benjamin Franklin's tombstone with their paper and crayons.

Within minutes, Lexi had broken the seal.

"Now for the fun part," Lexi said with a grin. "Are either of you scared of skeletons?"

"Um, yes," said Caleb.

"Also yes," said Maddie.

"Dang it, me too," said Lexi. "I was hoping one of you was going to be the brave one this time."

Maddie gulped. "What exactly do we hope to find in Ben Franklin's grave?" she asked. She hadn't considered yet what they would do if there was only a body under the slab. Up until this point, she had been certain they would find the next clue in their search for the Statue of Liberty.

"Oh boy," Caleb said, looking queasy as Lexi lifted the giant slab a few inches off the ground. They peered inside.

Sure enough, instead of layers of dirt, or a grave, or even a skeleton, there was a crumbling flight of stone steps descending into darkness.

"Whoa," Caleb said.

"Quickly," Maddie said. "We don't want anyone to walk by and catch us."

Lexi pushed the slab a few inches further, and Maddie and Caleb slipped underneath and began their descent. Lexi was close behind them, the giant slab thudding shut. The darkness was all-consuming, and they used their hands to feel their way forward, recoiling whenever they brushed cobwebs with their fingers. Maddie took out her phone to use the flashlight. She paused briefly before turning it on to consider what she might see. *Whatever we find in this basement will lead us closer toward Obscuritas, the Statue of Liberty, and the mastermind of evil, Doug.*

Maddie was just about to switch on her flashlight when a voice rang out, scaring her so much, she dropped her phone.

"Finally," the voice said. "I wondered when you would find me."

CHAPTER 25

Ex libris
From the library

The three agents froze. A rival agent? Someone from Obscuritas? Who else would have lured them to discover the secret chamber below Benjamin Franklin's grave? Maddie's heart raced. *Should we run ahead or back the way we came?* It was so dark, she wasn't sure which way was which, anyway.

A second later, a light flicked on. Maddie and her friends had reached the bottom of the stairs. As soon as their eyes adjusted, Maddie, Caleb, and Lexi got their first look at their enemy, standing on the floor of a dusty room.

"Hi, I'm Doug," he said, waving and holding a battery-powered lantern.

He was a boy—shorter than all of them—who appeared

to be about nine years old. "*You're* Doug?" Lexi asked in disbelief.

The notorious Doug was wearing jeans and a blue T-shirt that said *Franklin Elementary*.

The three agents exchanged looks, still frozen on the stairs.

"You're *Doug*?" Caleb asked again.

"Yes, I am Doug," the boy replied.

"You're *the* Doug?" Maddie asked.

"Yep! At least I think I am!" said the boy, smiling widely.

"Obscuritas Doug?" Lexi asked skeptically.

"Yes, I—wait, who?" the boy said. "I'm Douglas Winkle. Who is Obscuritas Doug?"

Their confusion must have been obvious, because Douglas Winkle, whoever he was, got defensive.

"Well, who are *you*?" he asked, also looking disappointed. "I thought you would be Illuminati. But you're just kids."

"So are you!" Lexi pointed out. "And besides, we—"

"Let's start over," Maddie gently interrupted. "Hi, Doug, I'm Maddie." Her tone was friendly and casual, as though they were meeting in an after-school club rather than in a secret lair under a cemetery. "You thought we would be Illuminati?"

"Yeah," Not-Obscuritas Doug said, a note of defensiveness in his voice again. "The Illuminati are real, you know. I've been studying them since I learned how to read. And I figured out how to get in here."

He lit another battery-powered lantern, and the agents took in their surroundings in more detail. The underground space was larger than it had seemed at first. There were tables and shelves covered in objects. They proceeded to the bottom of the stairs and began looking around.

"This is Ben Franklin's secret workshop," Not-Obscuritas Doug continued proudly. "He had more inventions and devices than most people ever knew about . . . um, be careful," he said as Lexi picked up a pair of glasses. "Those are bifocals that show multiple wavelengths at once. Ben's inventions were much more advanced than he was willing to reveal in public."

Maddie figured this kid got a pass for calling Benjamin Franklin "Ben," since he'd discovered his secret workshop and all. She was examining a silver key that she had removed from a glass-front cabinet and realized with a start that it was *the* key—the one Franklin had used to conduct electricity in his famous kite experiment. She gasped in awe.

"Your friends and family must have been very excited when you told them about this place," Caleb said, taking after Maddie and keeping his tone light. He was leafing through an ancient-looking notebook filled with symbols that looked like codes.

"Oh, no." Doug was appalled. "I haven't told anyone. That would violate the sacred trust of the Illuminati."

"You told us," Lexi pointed out as she set down the glasses with a *thunk* that made the rest of them wince.

"Oh yeah." Doug reddened a bit. "But you found me . . . wait, how did you find me?"

The three agents looked at each other. *Trust your instincts,* Maddie remembered from Zander's note. Maybe this kid was an Obscuritas plant . . . but Maddie really didn't think so. There was something genuine about him, in the way he talked about the Illuminati and cared for everything in the workshop.

"We went to Monticello," she said.

"Ah." Doug nodded. "Anywhere before that?"

Maddie paused. "The Smithsonian American Art Museum."

Doug clapped his hands together. "Oh! I wondered who would find those nickels I left at the museum!" He gestured at the small Statue of Liberty, which was propped in the corner. "But I was kind of hoping the Illuminati would find them. That's why I did it—to meet the Illuminati!"

Maddie glanced again at Caleb, and then at Lexi. They both nodded. *Trust each other.*

"Well, Doug," Maddie said, "we *are* the Illuminati."

Doug's jaw dropped. Before he could respond, they heard muffled sounds above. "Oh shoot, I lost track of time!" he said, grimacing. He scrambled to turn off the lanterns. "I always get out of here before the cemetery groundskeeper arrives, so that he doesn't hear me moving around down here."

"What should we do now?" Caleb asked.

"There's a back way out of here. Another tunnel," said Doug. "Follow me!"

Maddie's heart sank. There had so much she hadn't explored in the workshop yet! She grabbed two extremely old notebooks from a nearby table. And instead of putting the key back in its case, she stuck it in her pocket.

At that precise moment, her stomach growled. Loudly. Everyone turned to stare at her. Then Lexi's did, too. The growls echoed through the chamber, floating up toward the entrance.

Everyone froze, hoping the groundskeeper above didn't hear their stomach sounds through the stone. "We should get out of here—and find some food?" whispered Doug.

Caleb stifled a giggle. "Maybe the groundskeeper will just think that Ben got super hungry in the afterlife."

CHAPTER 26

Astra inclinant, sed non obligant.
The stars incline us, they do not bind us.

Doug led them out of the chamber, into a narrow hallway covered in newspaper clippings, all letters from a woman named Silence Dogood. "This was Ben Franklin's alter ego," he said, reverently running his hands down the yellowing photocopied pages, all showing old-fashioned print and the words *New-England Courant.*

"He wanted to get published in his brother's newspaper, so he pretended to be a widow named Mrs. Dogood to hide his identity. How cool is that?"

Maddie nodded politely at Doug's visible excitement.

The floor began to slant gently upward, and a few shafts of light illuminated dust motes just overhead.

"So, I actually haven't used this exit before," Doug said, a bit sheepishly. "I can't quite . . ." He raised his arms, still three feet beneath the cellar door above him.

"I got you!" said Lexi, already bending down to lift Doug by his legs. Before he could say anything, she'd given him a boost, and he tried to push the door open, his skinny arms straining. "Want me to try?" said Maddie.

"I can do it!" Doug grunted, and finally swung the door open with a heavy scraping noise. He flashed a triumphant look down at the agents, then scampered up over the ledge. Lexi boosted Caleb (who reminded everyone again that he did *not* like to be carried) and Maddie, and then swung herself up expertly by her fingertips, with a swoosh of her blue hair.

They found themselves in an alleyway, connecting to a busy street with shops and restaurants.

"I know where we are!" said Maddie. "Follow me."

They walked into a small storefront with *Famous Steaks* painted over the windows in bold red and white letters. A crowd of people stood at the counter, ordering cheese-steaks and sandwiches. The scent of frying onions and freshly baked bread wafted over them, and Maddie's stomach rumbled again. "I think Zander would approve of us using some of our cash to buy lunch, right?" she asked, a hopeful gleam in her eye.

Caleb nodded. "We can't be expected to find the Statue of Liberty on an empty stomach, now, can we?" he said.

They ordered cheesesteaks and then hustled back out to the alleyway with their sandwiches so as not to be overheard. With their voices low, they explained to Doug that they had recently joined the Illuminati. "This is actually our first mission," Maddie told him.

They gave him the highlights about their recruitment, their training at Camp Minerva, and the theft of the Statue of Liberty. Doug's eyes got wider and wider, until they looked like they might just pop out of his head.

"That's why we went to the Smithsonian," Caleb explained. "To see if there were any clues."

"Whoa," Doug said. "And you found *my* nickels, which led you to Ben Franklin's message at Monticello. It's like I'm part of a real Illuminati legend."

Maddie took a bite of her sandwich and closed her eyes, letting the melted cheese and perfectly thin slices of meat fill her mouth with deliciousness. Even though the sandwiches served at Camp Minerva were good, nothing could ever replace the real thing. The other kids agreed: these sandwiches were out of this world.

While they chowed down, Doug unrolled a grubby dollar bill from his pocket. "Check this out! You said you were trained at Camp Minerva? Minerva's symbol, the owl, is right *here*!" He pointed to the large numeral one on the upper right-hand corner of the bill. "See the tiny owl, right there by the border? It means wisdom."

Lexi peered closely at the tiny owl. "So this means

someone from the Illuminati designed the dollar bill?" she asked.

Doug nodded with a proud smile on his face. "Yep—and their influence is everywhere! Did you know the Washington Monument is an Illuminati beacon? And did you know, an Illuminati secret is the *real* reason the Liberty Bell is cracked. . . ."

As she listened to Doug's legends with half an ear, Maddie flipped through Ben Franklin's notebooks, noticing his graceful penmanship, detailed schedules, and schematic drawings. He had so much secret knowledge. Maddie realized with wonder that he was the *first* American Illuminati inventor! She reached into her pocket and looked down at the key she'd taken from the secret workshop, feeling a kinship with another inventor across the centuries. *I bet this thing is good luck,* she thought. First Benjamin Franklin, then Zander Lyon, and now her. She felt like she was part of something truly special, a line of noble inventors whose work was meant to change the world.

"Your knowledge of the Illuminati is impressive," said Caleb, "and, frankly, a little scary. What makes you so excited about this stuff?"

Doug put down his sandwich, then wiped his chin with the back of his hand. "Why wouldn't I be totally obsessed with the Illuminati? The Illuminati are like the most powerful secret organization in the world. You're real-life spies, hiding in plain sight! And, I gotta say, having kids as recruits—it's genius! I mean, no one would suspect kids!

"Also," he continued, eyes downcast, "I started an Illuminati club at my school, you know, to do research or whatever, but nobody joined."

"Well, now you're friends with the real thing," said Caleb.

Doug broke out into a little dance. "OH, YEAH, THE ILLUMINATI ARE REAL! AND THEY'RE MY FRIENDS!" he sang way too loudly. Lexi put her hand over Doug's mouth.

"*Hiding* in plain sight, remember?" she said.

"Wait a second, hiding in plain sight . . ." Suddenly, Maddie had a lightbulb moment. "If the members of Obscuritas were former Illuminati agents, that means they would know all about—and maybe even have access to— Illuminati technology." It was so obvious that she couldn't believe she hadn't thought of it before. "Maybe Obscuritas didn't *steal* the Statue of Liberty, maybe they just . . . invisibilized it!"

Lexi and Caleb stared at her. Maddie chewed the last bite of her sandwich, thinking hard. If she were to try to make something that large invisible, how would she do it? What kind of invention would it take? "Maybe they used some kind of cloaking technology—like the Illuminati use on their flying cars!"

"Maddie!" Caleb exclaimed. "That makes so much more sense. But to cloak something of that size . . ." He looked off into the distance, calculating. "Where's that ancient cell phone? Let's call Zander and tell him."

Just then, Maddie's super-tricked-out cell phone started buzzing. She answered it.

A familiar voice was on the other end. "Confirm location, agents," Volkov's icy voice rang out. "I need you to rendezvous with me ASAP."

"We're in Philly," said Maddie. "And we're headed to Liberty Island."

Volkov breathed in sharply. "What exactly do you think you're doing?"

Maddie paused—how much should she tell Volkov? For all Maddie knew, Volkov could be a secret member of Obscuritas!

"We need to talk to Zander," Maddie said instead.

"He is . . . unavailable right now," Volkov replied. "He cannot be disturbed."

While Maddie listened, Caleb fumbled with the old-fashioned clamshell phone.

"CALL HIM!" Maddie mouthed, pointing at his phone. Caleb dialed Zander, giving a thumbs-up when the line connected.

"Uh, hello, Mr. Lyon," Caleb said. In a quiet voice, he started to update Zander on everything they'd figured out so far. "At the Smithsonian, we found eight nickels. . . ."

"Maddie," said Volkov, "there are dangerous forces at play here. I need you to tell me everything that you and the other agents are up to. What do you know? Tell me!"

"What? Sorry, bad connection!" Maddie crinkled her sandwich wrapper by the phone and hung up abruptly.

Something strange was going on. Why was Volkov lying to Maddie? Zander clearly was available—he was on the phone with Caleb right then and there.

Caleb put his phone on speaker as he finished explaining everything to Zander. "So, we think Obscuritas didn't *steal* the Statue of Liberty. We think they just invisibilized it!"

On the other end of the line, there was a long silence. Finally, Zander's voice crackled through. "A fascinating hypothesis. Hmm."

Maddie and the other agents grinned at each other.

"Agents, I'm ordering all of you back to Illuminati headquarters at Camp Minerva immediately," Zander said.

Suddenly, the grins fell from their faces.

"But why?" asked Maddie. *We're so close to discovering Obscuritas and saving the day!*

"Because it's too dangerous for junior agents such as yourselves. I'll take an elite team to investigate this lead myself."

"But—" Maddie protested.

"You three have done great work, but now it's time to let those with more experience bring this to a close," he said.

"Wait, Mr. Lyon—" Caleb cried. Lexi just frowned. Maddie could tell from the looks on their faces that they wanted to see this mission through just as much as she did.

"That's an order, agents," Zander said firmly, and clicked off.

It was no use. Zander Lyon had given an official order.

An order to do exactly nothing.

CHAPTER 27

Sapere aude.
Dare to be wise.

They slumped against the brick wall of the alleyway, staring into their empty sandwich wrappers. Nobody moved. Doug took a sad sip of a root beer float he'd gotten to go.

All three agents began to speak at the same time.

"It just seems—" Maddie said.

"Why would—" Lexi said.

"Something's off—" Caleb said.

They looked at each other. They looked at Not-Obscuritas Doug. "What's going on?" he said.

"Exactly," Maddie said. "What *is* going on? Why would Volkov say Zander was unavailable when Caleb just talked to him?"

"He gave us an order," Caleb said. "We have to follow it."

Lexi cracked her knuckles. "Well, yeah—principle number one, 'Obey all orders from ranking Illuminati leadership.'"

Maddie fiddled with the silver key in her pocket. She always thought better when she was doing something with her hands. She wanted to follow the principles she'd agreed to, but she also really wanted to find the Statue of Liberty—because it was the right thing to do, but also, to prove that she could. Finding the missing torch-bearing statue seemed to line up perfectly with principle number three, *Let the light show the way*. In a way, the Statue of Liberty's light was *her* light. It felt like her responsibility to make it right again. And something about Volkov's tone—gruff and tense, rather than just plain old gruff—gnawed at her.

Caleb's face took on that detached, half-lidded look he got when he was trying to work out a puzzle. "What if there's more? What did that note from Zander say?"

Maddie rummaged through her nylon fanny pack, brought out a crumpled piece of paper, and read, "'Trust each other. Trust your instincts. You can do this.'"

"Wait a second. Isn't that an order, too?" Lexi said.

Maddie nodded. "In that note, Zander is telling us we need to trust each other and our instincts. And my instinct is telling me that something's fishy."

"Agreed," said Caleb, beginning to pace.

Maddie furrowed her brow. "What if . . . ," she thought

aloud. "What if Volkov is a mole? What if she's part of Obscuritas?"

Caleb suddenly stopped moving and looked at Maddie, his eyes wide. "That would explain why she lied on the phone call."

"And why Zander has been so cryptic this entire time," Maddie added.

"And why Volkov insisted on taking us out of the Empire State Building, instead of Archibald Archibald," Lexi said emphatically.

But Maddie remembered something else too. "I just told Volkov that we were heading to Liberty Island. If we're right, won't she realize that Zander is heading there now and alert Obscuritas that he's coming? He could be walking into a trap!"

Caleb nodded vigorously. "We have to get to him before they do. We need to save Zander Lyon!"

Suddenly, Maddie noticed that the four of them were on their feet, huddled together in excited anticipation.

"This is the mission we've been training for, super spies!" she said. "We can do this—can't we?"

"YES!" Not-Obscuritas Doug yelled, pumping his fist.

An elderly couple in matching tracksuits power-walking past the alleyway looked curiously toward the outburst, eyebrows raised. Maddie smiled apologetically. Then they all stared at Doug, who was bouncing lightly on his feet.

"I mean, if I have a vote," Doug whispered.

Maddie didn't think that Doug should come along, but the more she thought about it, the more it made sense. He already knew everything about the mission and who they were. Plus, he had buckets of knowledge about history and Illuminati lore, which could be very helpful in solving future clues. And she could tell he was trustworthy.

"Won't your parents miss you if you come with us?" she asked.

"Nope!" he said cheerfully. "My parents think I'm at summer camp. And summer camp thinks I stayed home with my parents this year!"

Caleb nodded, impressed. "Pretty bold move."

Doug blushed. "So are we going, or what?"

"I'm in," Caleb said.

"You know I'm in," said Lexi.

"Well, that settles it," Maddie said, grinning. She hated to leave Philadelphia without at least saying hello to Jessica and Jay, but duty called. "Lady Liberty, here we come!"

CHAPTER 28

Magna celeritate

With great speed

They hurried back to the garage where they'd parked their flying car. They raced up the stairwell to the top floor. Doug was bent over panting next to the maroon minivan, looking around the parking deck with a confused expression on his face.

"Well, where is it?" Doug asked, finally catching his breath.

Lexi pointed to the van and winked.

Doug looked at her. "You're kidding." Caleb shook his head, smiling.

"It's not even a hybrid!" Doug exclaimed. "And I don't see any Illuminati symbols. . . ."

Caleb gently tapped the hood ornament. It was a dull

gold triangle. Very discreet. "It's supposed to blend in," he said. He pointed to a sticker on the back window: *Save the Owls,* with a drawing of two eyes and a beak, in gold over a pea-green background.

Doug's eyebrows jumped up to his hairline. "Of course! That's so Illuminati."

As the four of them piled into the van, Caleb and Lexi silently pointed out the built-in mini-fridge, which offered every flavor of seltzer to Doug as they buckled him into his seat.

They needed to get to Liberty Island—and fast—but with the Statue of Liberty missing, it was the most-watched crime scene in the world.

The three agents puzzled over their next step, hovering somewhere above eastern Pennsylvania, while Doug continued to freak out about the invisible car.

"I think we need to call Sefu," Caleb said.

"Hey, did you know that if you press the strawberry seltzer button three times in a row on the minibar control panel, strawberry frozen yogurt comes out?" Doug said, his mouth full of the delicious treat.

Maddie smiled, then dialed Sefu, who, again, she woke up suddenly.

"Sefu," said Maddie on the car's speakerphone. "We need to get to Liberty Island, but security will be extra tight. They'll be on the lookout for anything coming in through the air."

"Of course," he said, yawning. "Let me just run your request by Commander Volkov, which should take only—"

"No!" said Maddie.

"Oh?" Sefu said, surprised.

"Both she and Zander told us to stay away."

"Then I cannot help you!" said Sefu. "I cannot disobey an order, you know that."

"But we also got a second order, directly from Zander, to trust our instincts, and our instincts say Zander is in trouble. We're trying to save him!"

"Hmm. Two opposing orders," said Sefu. There was a pause. "Okay, if it's for Zander, then I will help." A few moments later, holo-screens appeared on their S.M.A.R.T.W.A.T.C.H.es. "I just sent you something I began studying about Liberty Island's schematics as soon as the statue disappeared. I think I found something you can use. . . ."

Maddie zoomed in on the map Sefu had sent. "There's an underwater entrance to Liberty Island!" she said.

"Yes! Near the Hudson River," Sefu explained. "There's a building there, an old Illuminati outpost. From inside the building, you will be able to access an underwater route to the island."

"Thanks, Sefu," Maddie, Lexi, and Caleb all said at once.

"Thank you, Sefuuuuu!" Doug yelled after them.

◆ ◆ ◆

Minutes later, they touched down near the edge of the Hudson River, in a small parking lot next to a warehouse-like building that looked like it could fall over at any time. The fading sign out front read, *Norman's Used Books: Buy, Sell, & Trade*.

Maddie looked at her map. "This is the place, supposedly."

The four of them got out and walked in tentatively. They were immediately hit by the scent of yellowing paperbacks. Thousands of them! Stacked from floor to ceiling in no discernible order. Marble busts of famous authors were strewn around haphazardly.

Maddie found a pathway through the books to the store's front counter. *This doesn't look like an Illuminati HQ . . . But isn't that the point?* she asked herself.

The man behind the counter was very tall, but he sat on a low stool, absentmindedly twirling his mustache, absorbed in a mystery novel that looked so tattered that Maddie was sure some of the pages were missing.

Maddie didn't know exactly what to say. "Um, hi," she began. "I'm looking for something . . . special?"

The man shifted in his seat without looking up from his book. Maddie caught a glimpse of the man's pet perched behind him—a spotted owl. "*How* special?" he asked.

"Very," said Maddie, now certain she was in the right place.

"Try the back," he replied. "Rare Books."

Maddie waved her team toward the back. After walking through a maze of stacks, they landed at a door to the Rare Books room. "This is a secret Illuminati HQ," said Maddie as she pushed the door open. "Be ready for anything."

Instead, the room looked like more of the same—paperbacks and author busts in random piles.

"Look," said Caleb, picking a bust off the floor. "It's our old friend Frances Hodgson Burnett." He placed the statue on top of a stack of books, when Burnett's face seemed to come to life, just like the statues in the island's Hall of Inspiration!

"Did you . . . know?" Lexi asked.

"No idea. Whoa," Caleb replied.

"Identification?" asked the statue.

Maddie smiled. "Maddie Robinson, agent of the Illuminati," she said confidently.

"Identity authenticated," said the statue. "Welcome, Agent Robinson."

With a creak, the entire room began to sink. "We're going down!" said Lexi.

They descended several stories below ground, and the room/elevator opened to a warehouse-like space full of gear. Maddie spotted a fleet of fluorescent yellow vehicles. Each looked like a cross between a Jet Ski and a stationary bike, with an air tank on the front. Perched on each vehicle were a scuba suit and a large, round helmet, marked with a discreet golden triangle.

"Jackpot," Maddie said. "Personal submarines."

They zipped themselves into the neoprene scuba suits, which fit over their clothes and smelled like rubber bands. They helped each other with their helmets and attached their oxygen tubes.

They lugged their vehicles off their stands, over to a

sealed round portal, outlined in orange, with a huge *X* and the phrase *Direct Access to Hudson River/Liberty Island.*

Not-Obscuritas Doug was busy muttering, "This is so cool," over and over again.

Maddie pushed the bright orange button next to the portal, and a Plexiglas wall rose up from the floor around them, sealing them off from the rest of the lair. Then the round portal rotated with a low groan. Layers of metal twisted, revealing a pattern of openings like a kaleidoscope. Water started trickling in the openings, then gushed forward in a froth of white as the openings grew wider.

"I knew being a super secret super spy was going to be fun," said Lexi. "But I didn't think it would be *this* fun." She reached out a fist bump to a nervous Caleb, who fist-bumped her back, smiling.

The water sloshed around their legs and personal submarines until they were completely submerged.

Maddie rotated her personal sub's handlebars forward, as if she were revving a dirt bike, and whooshed out into the depths of the river, followed by Lexi, Caleb, and Doug.

"THIS IS AWESOME!" Doug yelled into their helmet communicator system.

If her device hadn't been stolen by an evil mastermind trying to kill her hero, Maddie might've agreed.

CHAPTER 29

Audentes fortuna iuvat.
Fortune favors the bold.

The three agents and Doug found themselves hovering in murky green water. Sediment from the river floor billowed around them in a beige swirl as the portal creaked shut behind them. Their helmets allowed access to their oxygen tanks and 360-degree visibility, but this deep, everything was gloomy and dark. Maddie wondered what was hiding in the depths beyond their visibility. She felt a shiver of fear, even though her scuba suit was insulated and temperature-controlled.

We can do this, she thought.

"Try to turn on your lights!" she said, pushing at random buttons on the control pad between the handlebars. Finally,

headlights clicked on the front of each personal sub, as well as a smaller one perched on the top of each of their helmets.

"Check this out!" Caleb called. "Push the green button with GPS on it." The others all did the same, and suddenly, an overlay of a map appeared inside their helmets. The map had simple red lines, with a compass in the corner, as well as indicators of depth, water pressure, and speed.

"We need to go south, and sort of east, as the crow flies—er, swims," Lexi said.

Maddie gave a clumsy thumbs-up with her neoprene-gloved hand. As she reached back down to grab her handlebar, she noticed a flashing neon-purple button on the left side of her keypad and pushed it. Suddenly, big-band jazz music poured into everyone's helmet, and a crooning male voice belted out, "Somewhere beyond the sea, somewhere waiting for meeeeeeee . . ."

The four of them burst into laughter, which helped ease their nerves.

"I'm plugging the coordinates of Liberty Island into our helmet-maps," Caleb said, using voice commands. They shot forward with a swoosh, swerving around huge cement blocks covered in barnacles. The cloudiness of the water cleared up slightly as they traveled farther from the lair, and the four of them had to use their subs' windshield wipers when plastic bags, bits of Styrofoam, and cigarette butts washed over them.

Maddie steered toward the right, following the bright red line on her helmet-map. A baseball floated by, and then a waterlogged loaf of bread, a broken umbrella, and a fancy gold watch, which Doug grabbed as they cruised by. "It might still work!"

"Keep moving!" Maddie said. "Our battery levels are already at fifty percent. I don't think these gizmos are usually meant to go this far." She thought back to training with piranhas at Camp Minerva. *Staying calm is the key,* she reminded herself.

"Did you know you can eat some kinds of seaweed?" Lexi asked as they navigated around pieces of wood, some as long as a whole tree. "Not as tasty as cucumbers, though. Whoa—look!"

They paused to watch a blue crab crawl slowly through the rocks beneath them.

"We're getting closer," Maddie said, consulting her map. "Keep an eye out for anything that looks like an entrance." She glanced nervously at her battery level, now blinking red at 25 percent. *It shouldn't be losing energy this fast.*

"It's almost like something is sucking the energy from our batteries," said Caleb.

Maddie gulped. That something might be . . . her Electrical Enhancer. If Obscuritas had gotten their hands on her device, they might already be using it to steal power for their own nefarious purposes. The agents needed to hurry.

They slowed their subs as they approached a wall of rock and cement. Carefully, they followed the wall until they reached a humongous, garage-like door. Maddie maneuvered her submarine close to a small yellow box that looked like a control panel. She looked down at her dashboard and her heart started racing. Her submarine's battery had just gone from 10 percent to 5 percent. They were running out of time. How was she going to hack into something underwater?

She looked at her helmeted friends, hovering in the water next to her. "Any ideas?" she said. Her battery level indicator clicked from 5 percent to 3 percent. If she didn't think of something soon, they were all going to drown.

She quickly reached out and flipped open the cover of the yellow box. There was a keypad underneath, with letters and numbers, like a phone. Maddie didn't have time to think. She punched in *OBSCURITAS* as fast as she could with her clumsy gloved fingers as the battery of her personal submarine turned red and started flashing: 0 percent.

They were out of time. For a brief moment, Maddie hoped she'd guessed the code correctly.

Just as their headlights began flickering, the massive underwater garage door began to open. Maddie's submarine started to sink. She dropped her handlebars and kicked with her legs as hard as she could to swim to the door. "Come on!" she yelled, hoping the others could still hear her.

Lexi, who was the strongest swimmer, kicked hard and shot forward inside the door. She reached down and grabbed Maddie, who reached out and grabbed Caleb, who grabbed Doug. With one final yank, Lexi pulled them all into the garage just as the huge door closed behind them with a definitive *SLAM!*

Maddie could hear her heart pounding in her ears, but they were through.

The water began to drain from the room, and the agents took in their surroundings. They were in a perfectly square chamber, completely tiled in white. A bright blue door sat in the center of each wall, not counting the garage door to the river behind them.

They peeled off the underwater gear, leaving them back in their regular clothes.

"That was close," said Caleb, breathing hard. "No more near-death experiences, please."

"Which way should we go?" asked Lexi.

"No idea. But I don't think we should linger in case our arrival set off some kind of alarm," said Maddie.

"We approached Liberty Island at ten degrees south by southeast, traveling at 12.2 knots. Thus, it stands to reason that the fastest way to the center of the island would be to take the door on the right. Sorry if that was obvious," said Caleb.

"Yeah . . . so obvious," said Lexi, smiling and shaking her head.

They opened the door on the right and found a long, empty corridor, also tiled in white, lit by yellowish bulbs that hung from the ceiling every few feet. It smelled damp and earthy.

They crept along the wall until the corridor branched, leading off in two different directions.

"Hmm, which way?" Maddie mused.

"Can you please remind me, what are we looking for?" Not-Obscuritas Doug whispered.

"We're trying to find out how Obscuritas made the Statue of Liberty invisible," Caleb said, in a calm, professor-like voice. "And reverse whatever they did."

"And take back my Electrical Enhancer," Maddie added.

"And hopefully kick some butts," Lexi chimed in.

Doug nodded. "Got it!" His eyes sparkled, and he gave an eager thumbs-up to the group.

Suddenly, a loud scream echoed from the corridor to the right. It sounded like a man. "I think that's Zander!" Maddie said.

"He's probably fighting Volkov," Maddie said, breaking into a run. "We have to help him!"

Lexi zoomed ahead. They ran down a long maze of hallways, following the pounding of Lexi's footsteps and the sounds of Zander screaming.

The end of the last hallway opened up into a large bunker. The cavernous room was several stories high, wrapped by several balconies. On the main floor, hundreds of fascinating yet rudimentary-looking machines belched out wisps of steam, surrounding rows of desks, papers piled high atop them. Dull metal robots with no heads sat at each desk, moving paper with their long, spindly arms and typing into machines that sort of resembled computers. Pipes jutted out from the walls and floor, occasionally emitting clouds of steam. The clacking of the metal robot fingers on the metal keyboards created a relentless sound, like a rainfall of pennies.

"I think we found Obscuritas's control center," Lexi whispered.

Maddie nodded and looked up. Flying dozens of feet above their heads, two men in Rocket Boots twisted and whirled, grappling and wrestling in an all-out brawl.

"It's Zander!" Caleb cried.

"And . . ." Maddie squinted at the other man in midair, now upside down and grabbing at the other man's boots. "Zander?"

Two identical faces. Two Zanders. And they looked like they were trying to tear each other apart.

CHAPTER 30

Ignotum per ignotius

The unknown by the more unknown

"There are *two* Zanders?" Doug said. "Now I'm really confused."

"One of them must be an evil Obscuritas agent in disguise!" Lexi guessed.

But who could match Zander blow for blow? Maddie wondered. "It must be Doug!" she exclaimed.

"Me?" Not-Obscuritas Doug placed a hand to his chest, looking shocked.

"No! The head of Obscuritas, Doug!" said Maddie. They had to figure out what to do, and fast. But how to know which Zander was which?

"Maybe if we call out his name, we'll know who is who by which one turns around," said Maddie.

"Zander!" Lexi hollered.

Both men paused their battle and simultaneously turned to look at the team of kids. It was clear that they'd just realized they had an audience. Both of the Zanders looked equally surprised.

"So much for that theory," Lexi muttered.

"Stay back, children!" one of the Zanders called out. "It's

worse than I thought! He will stop at nothing to get what he wants!" This Zander seemed worried—his eyebrows were furrowed, and he sounded truly concerned. But was he just acting? There was no way to tell if he was tricking them.

Just then, that Zander was thrown backward into the wall and collapsed in a heap into a corner of the room, apparently out cold. The other Zander had taken advantage of the distraction and was now wiping the sweat from his face.

"Agents!" the sweaty, still-conscious Zander said, hovering about ten feet in the air. "How did you access this facility? I thought you were heading back to headquarters, as I ordered."

This must be the real Zander! Maddie turned and lifted her chin, just a bit. "We were, but then we realized that you were in danger. Volkov was on her way to stop you. We think she's an Obscuritas spy."

Caleb and Lexi stepped forward to join her.

"And we thought you might need backup," Maddie continued. The three of them beamed at Zander, proud that they'd helped him beat the other, evil Zander. Maddie couldn't believe that they'd actually accomplished their mission. They'd found Obscuritas and saved Zander, just like they set out to do.

"You're even more clever than I gave you credit for. Maybe even as smart as me? Who knows! Now we just have to do something about that guy." Zander jerked his head in the direction of his passed-out doppelgänger.

"Can you secure him? And make sure he's really out?" he asked them.

"Sure thing," Maddie said. The three agents and Doug tentatively crept toward the corner of the room, where the other Zander lay in a heap.

Lexi prodded evil Zander's leg with her foot. It moved like a rag doll. He didn't stir.

"He's out," she confirmed.

"Whew," Maddie said. She headed back toward the real Zander and *BLAM!*—she slammed face-first into an invisible wall. Maddie was stunned. *What is happening?* she thought.

Zander smiled at them from across the room. Not smiled. Smirked.

"Sorry," he said. "Like I said, you really are very clever. Unfortunately, you're also meddlesome. Which is why I need you out of the way, and my invisible force field will help with that." His smirk made Maddie's blood run cold.

"What the . . . ," Lexi sputtered. She took a flying ninja kick at the invisible wall in between them and Zander, but it was no use. Caleb pressed his hand to the wall, testing it. It wouldn't budge.

They were trapped.

CHAPTER 31

Cui bono?
Who benefits?

"You let us out right now!" Lexi demanded. Zander laughed maniacally, his face no longer sweaty. He looked cool and calm, as if he hadn't just been fighting a look-alike in midair moments ago.

"You're not going anywhere," he said. "You're done! This handsome but annoying thorn in my side is defeated, and I have your invention. Now I can be in control, just like I always planned."

"Wha-what do you mean?" asked Maddie.

"The Statue of Liberty was built to cover up what the Illuminati were really building on Bedloe's Island: a secret energy harvester, designed to collect all the world's raw energy and then give it away for free. But the tech was only theoretical! The device to collect energy wirelessly didn't exist. Until your Electrical Enhancer, Maddie."

"No!" Maddie yelled.

"That's right," Zander hissed. "*You* built the device that will let me take over the world! I'll control the world's energy supply, and everyone—EVERYONE!—will have to obey me if they want any little smidgen of it."

Maddie and her friends were dumbfounded. This didn't sound like the Zander they knew, who was always inventing eco-friendly gadgets and creating initiatives to help save the world.

"Zander, you don't sound like yourself," said Lexi.

"He's got to be joking," added Caleb.

"You never wanted to light the torch forever," Maddie said slowly, as the reality dawned on her that Zander was not a good guy. In fact, he sounded a lot like a bad guy.

"Of course not," Zander laughed. "Technology that powerful . . . for some glorified lighthouse? Just to be a symbol of what . . . Freedom? Democracy? Enlightenment?" He spat out the last word like it disgusted him. Then he laughed so hard that he snorted like a pig. Which would have been funny in normal circumstances, but not while they were trapped behind a force field by a madman.

"Thank you for figuring out that Obscuritas rendered the statue invisible," he noted. "They guessed my plan and made the whole thing invisible just so I couldn't get to it!

But now that I'm here, I can finally enact my plan and take down Obscuritas once and for all."

"And then what?" asked Maddie, fighting back tears.

"*And then what?*" Zander said mockingly. "And then I'll use your Electrical Enhancer to steal power from all over the globe. I'll sell it back to the highest bidder! Quick Zan-ecdote for you: doing things for the good of humanity, hiding our accomplishments—you know, the whole Illuminati shtick—it's a crock of stinky stuff. Now it's time for me to get some credit, and some cash, for my genius!" He let loose an evil-sounding giggle.

"You'll never win," Not-Obscuritas Doug piped up. "Not with these guys fighting you."

"Is this Bring Your Little Brother to Work Day? Who is this pipsqueak?" Zander asked, annoyed. "You know, it doesn't matter. I have what I need from you already." His face darkened. He looked right at Maddie. "And once I've started using your device to steal the world's energy, I'll be back to finish you off."

With that, he blasted off in his Rocket Boots. Up, up, up he flew through the atrium, past the robots, and the steam pipes and the balconies, what looked like twenty stories up to an escape hatch at the top of the room.

With a single fluid motion, Zander flipped forward in midair and blasted the hatch open with a rocket-powered kick. He disappeared into the night sky.

"Show-off," Lexi muttered.

"I know he's trying to kill us, but that was the coolest thing I've ever seen," said Caleb.

Maddie might've laughed at Caleb's observation, if it wasn't for the fact that her hero, Zander Lyon, wasn't a hero at all. He was a villain. And he had just blasted off to enact his evil plan.

CHAPTER 32

Per ardua ad astra

Through adversity to the stars

"I don't know who that guy was, but I'd really like to get out of here before he comes back," said Doug, scared.

Maddie gave Caleb and Lexi a look. Doug was right—they could *not* wait for Zander to return. He was totally unhinged.

The other Zander began to stir. They all huddled around him. Lexi assumed a karate-fighting stance. His eyes flickered open.

"Hi, I'm Doug," he said, with a weak smile.

"You're Doug?" Maddie asked. She felt like she'd already had this conversation once.

"Yup," said the man. "Doug Lyon."

"Wait, what?" Maddie knew everything there was to know about Zander Lyon. She'd read his autobiography over a dozen times. She knew that he was lactose intolerant and had built his first bicycle before he'd even learned how to ride. But she'd never known that he had a brother.

"Twin brother," Doug sighed, by way of explanation.

"Whoa," Caleb said.

"How can we trust that you're telling the truth? This could be a disguise," said Lexi. She pulled at his cheeks, stretching them as far out as they would go. And then she pulled at his ears and hair. It all stayed firmly in place.

Then Maddie took a step closer and looked into his eyes. They were sadder than Zander's. Kinder. "You're telling the truth," she suddenly realized. She sat down next to him.

"Nice to meet you, Doug," she said. "I'm Maddie. We need you to tell us everything."

He told them the story of Obscuritas. "We used to be Illuminati members . . . until Zander was put in charge."

Maddie shrugged. "I guess you could tell he was a jerk way before we figured it out."

"Zander was good once," Doug continued. "But he slowly turned away from the Illuminati's purpose: helping people and guiding the world without taking credit. Zander grew corrupted by his fame and fortune."

"You saw what was happening to him . . . ," said Caleb.

"So did a lot of people—but Zander expelled everyone who opposed him. So we formed Obscuritas, to stop Zander and to return the Illuminati to its rightful mission."

Maddie's head was spinning. "So the rogue agents of Obscuritas are actually the good guys!"

"Zander was obsessed with a long-forgotten Illuminati plan to use the Statue of Liberty as an energy harvester, but I knew he wanted to use it for his own gain." Doug gestured to the facility they were trapped inside. "I've been working here with the agents of Obscuritas, keeping a watchful eye on Lady Liberty, ever since.

"As soon as we learned about the Electrical Enhancer," the No-Longer-Notorious Doug went on, nodding at Maddie, "we cloaked the Statue of Liberty, so Zander couldn't redirect her power for his own terrible goals."

"But how did you know—" Maddie's head was spinning. The only people who knew about the Electrical Enhancer and the Statue of Liberty were Maddie, Caleb, Lexi, and . . .

"Killian?!" Caleb asked, dumbfounded.

"No way," Obscuritas Doug said. "I hear that kid's a total punk."

"Volkov," Maddie said. Volkov *had* been an Obscuritas spy all along. But they'd gotten it all wrong. She was on the good side. Maddie was going to have some apologizing to do if they all made it through this alive.

"Of course!" Caleb smacked his forehead. "That explains why she 'accidentally' dropped those keys back at the Empire State Building—she wanted us to take her car. She was trying to help us!"

And all the while, Zander had been trying to slow

them down and get them out of the way.

"Unfortunately, you're not the only ones who have figured that out," Obscuritas Doug told them. "Zander and his minions will want to get rid of anything—and anyone—they consider to be blocking their path to domination. I'm afraid she and the other Obscuritas sympathizers are in danger."

No. Maddie wouldn't let Zander use her device to take over the world. *This is my responsibility,* she thought. She was determined to escape and take Zander down.

She touched Benjamin Franklin's key inside her pocket and, inspired by the Illuminati inventor, became determined to think her way out of their prison. Suddenly, she had an idea.

"Does anyone have a coin?" she asked. "Or another small object?"

Lexi produced a mint she had taken from the storefront. "Let me know if you need more," she said. "I grabbed at least five of them."

Maddie tried to toss the mint up and over the force-field wall. It made a zapping sound and fell back down.

"Let me try," Lexi said.

They waited while she did some stretches, and then she threw the mint. It sailed up and then finally came down . . . but on the other side of the wall.

"That's what I thought," Maddie said. "That's what I need to do."

The group was reluctant, because they didn't want Maddie to be flattened like a pancake when she hit the ground on the other side of the wall. But Maddie remembered there was an unusual-looking ball of twine in the fanny pack—a length of nano-diamond rope as thin as dental floss. If it was as strong as the other Illuminati materials, maybe they could lower her down on the other side.

With their best approximation of circus performers, they managed to boost Maddie up, and she pulled herself over the top of the invisible wall. Using the rope, the team worked together to lower her down safely.

Maddie turned back to the rope. "All right, who's next?" asked Maddie.

"Go get Zander!" Lexi and Caleb cried out at the same time.

She looked at her friends for a moment, then nodded. She raced back to the personal submarines. They required a few adjustments. Using the tools in the fanny pack and her own knowledge from years of tinkering in her cousin's laundry room, she began taking apart the personal submarines and sorting the parts.

"Zander wants to use my machine to take over the world?" Maddie asked as she pulled up 3D schematics of the personal subs on her S.M.A.R.T.W.A.T.C.H. "Then I'll use his own machines to stop him."

Using the parts from her fanny pack—the rope, the miniature drills, the smart-plastics—she reconfigured and enhanced the propellers from the submarines and pointed them upward. She looked for a way to join two pieces together and found the gum Zander had given them.

"Zanecdote: 'You never know when you'll need gum,'" Maddie repeated, sticking the gum to her invention.

The lighter payload and now-extra-powerful fans had transformed the three subs into a sleek vehicle built for one. She grabbed hold of her personal submarine, which was no longer a submarine—now it was a personal helicopter.

Maddie's heart was pounding as she lifted the copter above her head and clicked it on. The blades whirred and the tiny helicopter lifted her off the ground in jerky movements as she learned to control the vehicle. "Whoa!" she yelled as she got the hang of the device. She flew through the hallways and back into the control room. Then she flew toward the escape hatch that Zander had used.

"I'm coming for you, Zander!" Maddie yelled as her friends cheered.

"Now, this is what I'm talking about!" said the younger, Not-Obscuritas Doug, as he exchanged a high five with Obscuritas Doug.

Maddie's invention climbed up, up, and carried her through the escape hatch.

Suddenly, she was flying into the night sky. Liberty Island grew smaller below, and Maddie clung to the mini-copter as tightly as she could. The only thing between her and the ground was a homemade aircraft. She decided not to look down anymore.

Maddie was confident her craft could take her all the way up to meet Zander at the Statue of Liberty's torch. If there was one thing she knew how to do in life, it was to make amazing inventions out of what others might dismiss as junk. She exhaled sharply as the danger of her mission finally hit her. She didn't know how she was going to succeed going toe-to-toe with her former hero.

It doesn't matter, she told herself. *I have to try.*

CHAPTER 33

Inveniam viam aut faciam.
Find a way, or make one.

Maddie zoomed up to the top of the Statue of Liberty. Pieces of the statue began popping in and out of view, like a glitching computer monitor.

If the statue was becoming visible again, it meant that Zander had figured out how to "un-invisibilize" it—and was moving forward with his evil plan.

Finally, at the base of the torch, Maddie saw Zander searching the surface for the Electrical Enhancer. When he saw her, she saw a small flicker of fear shoot across his face and then disappear. Wind whipped Maddie's hair into her face as she swung and lurched in the air on her homemade helicopter closer and closer to the torch, though Zander's stayed perfectly gelled in place.

Before she could land, her helicopter started rattling and shaking. "Help!" she cried out.

Zander only smirked, not offering any help, as Maddie swung desperately from the sputtering aircraft, flinging herself onto the deck of the torch just in time. She clung to a rail, catching her breath, as the mini-copter ran out of juice and crashed behind her. She felt her cell phone fall out of her pocket and knew it was falling hundreds of feet to the rocks or the water below. She tried to grab it with her free hand, but it was too late. *No!*

She hoisted herself up on the railing and dropped over the edge, landing in a crouch.

Zander spotted the Electrical Enhancer and detached it from the torch. He aimed the device at the island of Manhattan and turned up the dial. Across the river, building lights began flickering, and one by one the skyscrapers went completely dark. Maddie just watched, still on her knees, in horror.

Zander took a step closer to her. "Oh, Maddie," he crooned. "You *should* be kneeling at my feet. Quick Zanecdote for ya: Zander always wins! Soon I'll be the richest, most famous, most powerful person in the history of the world. What do you think they'll call me? King Zander? Zander the Great? That's got a nice ring to it, doesn't it?"

Maddie took a deep breath. Without her phone, she had no way to use the flash to blind Zander, or use the extra-powerful vibration motor she'd added to knock him off his feet. *That means I have to outsmart him.*

"That's the thing," Maddie said as casually as she could muster. "I've come to join you. I thought about what you said. You're right that being ignored stinks. I've been ignored my whole life! At school! On the playground. Even at the science competition, with their made-up awards! I deserve more than that."

Zander regarded her warily, so she continued.

"I have more technology than just that Electrical Enhancer," Maddie said. "Why should it go to waste when I could join the most powerful person in the world?"

The moment the words were out of her mouth, she knew that her flattery had worked. A huge smile formed on Zander's lips, and he offered his hand to help her stand. But Maddie wasn't looking at his outstretched hand. She was looking at the other, the one holding the Electrical Enhancer.

She lunged toward it, and once she had it in her grasp, she looked up at him with determination in her eyes.

"Give me that!" he cried, trying to jerk it away, but it was no use. Maddie held it tight to her chest so Zander couldn't grab it. Using his Rocket Boots, he rose a few feet off the ground and flew straight at Maddie. In an instant, Maddie aimed her Enhancer at Zander's boots and stole all their juice, sending him skidding along the torch's base.

"You stupid girl!" Zander shouted. "How dare you take power from me?"

"That's just the thing, Zander." She looked at her Electrical Enhancer. "It's a two-way device. So if you want some more power for your boots, I'd be happy to help."

"No!" Zander shouted. He knew Maddie's plan—but he was too slow to stop her. Maddie flipped a switch on the Enhancer and pointed it at Zander's boots. He looked down with horror as his boots flicked on, out of his control, launching him ten feet in the air. He bicycled his arms and legs, trying to get closer to the torch, reaching wildly to grab on to anything he could.

Maddie set the Electrical Enhancer to full power. Now bursting with energy, the Rocket Boots shot Zander up, up, up into the night sky. He went flying over the Hudson River until he became just a speck in Maddie's vision.

"Maaaaadddddddiiieeeeee!" he squealed as the boots finally malfunctioned several miles over the Hudson River, sending Zander plummeting into the water.

Maddie sighed. Then wiped a tear. Then let out a long, well-deserved sigh.

She reached into her pocket and wrapped her hands around Ben Franklin's lucky silver key. Maddie couldn't believe she'd actually done it. She'd actually saved the world.

CHAPTER 34

Esse quam videri
To be, rather than to seem

Just two days later, all the Illuminati agents worldwide—new recruits, junior and senior-level agents, all the way up to top Illuminati leadership (including several heads of state, famous scientists, writers, and even a few pop stars)—were called to report to the Empire State Building headquarters on the hundredth floor for a special ceremony before the end of the summer. And it all had to do with Maddie's latest invention.

Everyone was given brand-new golden robes before the event. Maddie zipped hers up, letting the silky softness envelop her. When she looked in the mirror, she looked different, but also the same. An inch or two taller, a whole lot stronger (inside and out), and just a *bit* tired around the eyes—she'd been busy inventing!

She grinned at herself in the mirror, sticking out her tongue. Under that fancy robe was the same brave, ingenious, make-it-work Maddie that she'd always been. Just with a few more (okay, a *lot* more) abilities and knowledge. Lexi twirled in her robe like a ballerina, and Caleb looked particularly pleased to be wearing his, even if it didn't have elbow patches.

The three of them lined up along with Sefu and Killian, who looked even more smug than usual in his golden robe. He had even accessorized it with a golden tie with an owl stitched in the center.

"Are we all supposed to be wearing those?" asked Maddie.

"No. I had this custom-made, from a very exclusive tailor in London," Killian sniffed.

As they readied themselves to proceed into the ceremony hall, Volkov appeared at Maddie's elbow. "I have some news, young agent," she whispered. She ushered Maddie through a hidden door into a sleek conference room wallpapered in golden triangles.

"The Illuminati's Inner Circle has ruled. Doug Lyon is to be reinstated in the Illuminati. And he will be the new CEO of LyonCorp."

"That's nice," said Maddie, not sure why Volkov had taken her aside to tell her.

"Doug will also be the public face of the Illuminati's newest gift to the world, your invention, the Solar Enhancer."

"Oh."

Maddie swallowed. Her face felt hot. It had been Maddie's idea to reverse her device and use solar power—along with Benjamin Franklin's superconductive silver key—to feed energy out into the world's electrical grid through a high-tech wireless network system that could even reach inaccessible locales, anywhere in the world.

The Solar Enhancer was *her* idea. *She'd* come up with the concept, and *she'd* built it. She opened her mouth to say something.

Volkov put a hand on her arm. "Maddie, I know it's hard," she said, almost not-gruffly. "So many Illuminati agents have made major achievements, moved humanity forward by great leaps and bounds, and not gotten any credit. We prefer to help guide the world to better things, unseen and unsung. I realize that's hard to swallow, especially for one so young." She sighed deeply. "You do understand it's for the greater good, don't you?"

Maddie thought for a minute, then nodded, slowly. She knew that everyone in the Illuminati—Doug, Volkov, all the recruits, Archibald Archibald, and even the highest-ranking Illuminati members around the world knew the Electrical Enhancer was her invention.

"There's a motto in the Inner Circle," Volkov said, glancing around the room, as if they were somehow possibly being overheard. "*Veritas vincit*. It means, 'the truth always prevails.'" And with that, she winked her jeweled eye and walked out of the conference room.

Maddie straightened her robes, took a deep breath, and followed Volkov into the ceremony hall. It was a grand ballroom with a soaring, arched ceiling, filled with golden garlands and lit only by fiery torches and thousands of candles.

There were dozens of round tables with white-and-gold tablecloths and the most unique, beautiful, and downright weird combinations of flowers as centerpieces. Platters of delicious-smelling food from every cuisine in the world were being served by TuxBots. Maddie reached out and grabbed a piping-hot samosa from one tray, a ceramic spoonful of miso soup from another, and a mini hamburger from yet another tray, popping them into her mouth with delight. She washed it all down with a flute of sparkling pomegranate juice.

She sat down at a table with Lexi and Caleb as some of the torches were dimmed. The signature Illuminati chime rang out from a gong. Everyone fell silent. The ceremony began.

Many secret rituals happened at this ceremony, all lit by candlelight, to a soundtrack of echoing gongs, ancient melodies, and some pretty decent tuba solos courtesy of Archibald Archibald. Secret words were spoken, secret oaths were made, secret dances were danced, and secret songs were sung.

Then, after the last ancient, secret rites were performed, Not-Obscuritas Doug was officially inducted into the Illuminati, as the youngest member in history. He beamed, bouncing lightly on his toes, as Doug and Volkov placed a specially hemmed golden robe around young Doug's shoulders and placed their hands on his head, uttering secret words. Volkov handed him a card to sign, pledging his allegiance to the Illuminati, as Maddie and the other agents had done. After signing, Doug put a hand up for a high five, but Volkov shook her head, then older Doug sneezed into his hand, so young Doug was forced to high-five himself.

"Agents," Volkov began, "we've gathered you here today to commemorate a historic event."

Lexi and Caleb looked over at Maddie with excitement in their eyes. She smiled back at them.

"We are pleased to introduce new technology that will change the world as we know it," Volkov continued. "Maddie Robinson's Solar Enhancer is truly a remarkable achievement. It soaks up solar rays and, utilizing the powerful energy vortex at the Statue of Liberty, will distribute free electricity to the entire world. The American press will unveil this groundbreaking technology later today, and its implementation will roll out in the coming months. Please join me in celebration to commemorate this historic moment."

Everyone cheered. Maddie was called up to the stage. Doug Lyon reverently presented her with a heavy gold medal, imprinted with a golden triangle on one side and the All-Seeing Eye on the other.

"This is for your great contribution to the Illuminati, and to humanity. When you see this medal, only you and other members will know what it *really* means. Well done, super spy." He winked, then looped the shining medal around her neck.

Everyone in the ballroom (even Killian, albeit a bit reluctantly) stood and clapped for Maddie. Lexi and Caleb hooted and yelled, and Doug was jumping up and down and raising the roof. Even the owls perched up above Maddie seemed to be looking down at her approvingly.

She smiled, feeling herself blush—she wasn't used to all this attention focused her way. Then she decided not to be embarrassed and just to enjoy the moment.

She thought about her parents—how proud they would be, not just for saving the world, but because she was becoming a world-class inventor and explorer, like they had been.

I swear I'll figure out what happened to them one day, no matter what it takes, she told herself.

Confetti shot out of cannons on either side of Volkov. It was party time!

TuxBots passed trays of cucumber sorbet served with fresh raspberries, mini apple fritters, and slices of Philadelphia cheesecake to honor Lexi's, Caleb's, and Maddie's contributions to stopping Zander's evil plan. The three of them and Doug danced and ate cheesecake until their feet were sore and their stomachs were full.

The next assignment for Maddie and her friends was a

tough one: to go home and pretend nothing was out of the ordinary, like they were just regular kids who had gone to a regular (but *very* exhausting) summer camp.

Maddie looked at her friends and beamed. She knew that there would be other bad guys and other dangerous missions ahead of them. But for now, she just pinched herself, because all was right in the world, and it was time to celebrate.

EPILOGUE

Nova ingressus
On to new adventures

Several weeks later, Maddie was happily back home in the Philadelphia apartment with Jessica and Jay—and even happier that the Illuminati had provided her with her own high-tech super secret lab, hidden in the back of a greasy muffler repair shop down the block.

She'd used this lab to develop a new type of super secret ultrathin composite to build herself a real bed, one that, with the flick of a switch, automatically slid out from under Jessica and Jay's couch. It was topped with a synthetic silk-like fabric bubble made out of recycled plastic that inflated to create a supersoft mattress. She used a few more slabs of the composite and some top secret gecko-foot-inspired adhesive, ultra-strong magnets, and an old remote control

241

from Mrs. Dubrow's cast-off TV set to create a chest of drawers that clung to the ceiling. With the push of a button, she could choose a drawer, make it descend to Maddie-level, and pick out what she wanted to wear, or easily put away fresh laundry.

No more sleeping on the couch for this super spy, with her belongings in a sad little pile on the floor. Jay acted like he wasn't impressed by Maddie's living room improvements, while Jessica was so blown away she made Maddie reorganize her closet with the same tech.

She didn't have her own cell phone anymore, since hers had plopped into the Hudson, so she couldn't call or text or use any mobile-based app. She considered building one—but she had a better idea. Email and instant messaging on public library or school computers was far too easy to track and trace.

So she figured out another solution. One so analog, so innocent-looking, that no one would even think that super secret Illuminati messages were being conveyed among four (uniquely talented) regular kids. They wrote letters—"snail mail," Caleb called it. Sent right through the US mail. Sure, she had to buy stamps, but that was a lot cheaper than a phone and a data plan. Maddie always decorated the outside of her envelopes with smiley faces and stars to make her letters seem even more innocuous—just some chatty little notes among pen pals. Caleb decorated his with stars and spaceships, and Lexi tended to draw flowers and plants. They had to talk to Doug about *not* drawing Illuminati symbols on his, or even cartoon owls. He finally decided on a key, as a nod to Ben Franklin.

In their snail mail, they shared what they were up to, news about their families, and what they were learning in school. Lexi always included the latest soil pH, yield levels, and planting progress on the cucumber farm. They shared book recommendations and goofy jokes. Those notes they wrote by hand in plain English.

They also shared their hopes, dreams, and ideas for Illuminati inventions and future missions when they'd all be together again someday at Camp Minerva. These letters utilized a secret code that only the four of them knew. They switched the code every two weeks, just to keep any interceptors confused, and to keep their code-generating skills sharp.

Maddie's most recent letter was a quick one:

Efbs Mfyj, Dbmfc, boe Epvh,

Uijt ofyu ujnf xf "cpsspx" Wpmlpw't dbs,

=) lopx xifsf J'n ubljoh ju: uif Opsui Qpmf.

Mpwf,

Nbeejf

But even with the letters, and her own super secret lab, and the comfort of watching movies at home with Jessica and Jay, Maddie still missed hanging out with her fellow agents, and being part of something larger than herself. Going back to her regular life (mostly) was okay, just a little less exciting. Actually, a lot less exciting.

One day in late September, Maddie wondered how she'd been back in school for a month already. Her teachers were fine, if somewhat ordinary compared with her mentors at Camp Minerva. Her classmates generally ignored her, as they had always done. Though to be fair, she was so busy with her lab, she hadn't tried very hard to make new friends.

That day, her teacher, Mr. Zahler, announced that the day's normal lessons were being been postponed, so the students could watch a history-making event, projected live on a screen at the front of the classroom.

Mr. Zahler dimmed the lights, and the class settled into their seats, whispering about what it could be and excited to be skipping their usual Monday Morning Math Quiz.

The intro for the local news blared out from the TV. A female newscaster with a bright-eyed grin announced that the Statue of Liberty was getting a major upgrade. A new, world-changing invention, the Solar Enhancer, would now take in solar rays—aka sunbeams—and use them to provide power for the entire world's electrical grid—for free!

According to the newscaster, Doug Lyon, the genius twin brother to recently missing CEO Zander Lyon, was responsible for this breakthrough. Ever since Doug had assumed the role of CEO at his brother's corporation, LyonCorp, he'd been hinting at a big development, and today was apparently the day he'd decided to officially release the news.

"Hey, nerd," whispered the obnoxious new kid who was sitting behind Maddie this year. "You think you're smart? That Doug is a *real* genius." Maddie wanted to turn around and tell him the truth. But instead, she laughed softly, reminding herself that *veritas vincit*—the truth always prevails. No one would ever know what she and her friends had accomplished. But Maddie didn't mind. She had set out to change the world. And she had.

The cameras turned to Doug, who stood on the balcony of the torch of Liberty Island. "Today, I'm turning on the world's first Multi-Accessible Dynamic Electricity grid, or as we're calling it," he said, looking right into the camera that was on the balcony with him, "the Mad-E grid."

Maddie's heart fluttered, and she grinned.

The Maddie grid, Maddie thought. *Veritas vincit.*

Maddie and her classmates watched an image of a crane lowering her machine onto the Statue of Liberty's torch. After the device was successfully attached to the torch, the television screen and the lights in Maddie's classroom flickered and went out. Then the lights came back on, maybe even a *smidgen* brighter than they were before.

Maddie's heart raced, and she couldn't help but let a huge smile spread across her face. Her invention was already working, on a global scale! The entire world would have free electricity forever!

The whole classroom clapped. At the front of the classroom, Mr. Zahler cleared his throat. "To mark this historic event, you will all now write an in-class, five-paragraph essay on what this invention means to you, and how you envision it changing the world—and math. You will have thirty minutes. But first . . . we have something new for the classroom."

Mr. Zahler lifted a huge cardboard box and plopped it on his desk with a grunt. The whole class sat forward in their seats, eager with anticipation.

"Thanks to an anonymous donation," said Mr. Zahler, "we've been given brand-new . . ."

"Laptops!" Maddie guessed.

"Tablets!" the obnoxious boy yelled.

"Puppies?" a hopeful-looking girl in pigtails shouted.

". . . math textbooks!" Mr. Zahler said sternly. Maddie and her fellow students groaned. "They're already stamped with your names. Come up and take your book when I call you."

Maddie waited for her name to be called. Her classmates earlier in the alphabet flipped through their new books with boredom in their eyes. When she finally got her book, Maddie opened to page one. To her shock, the first page had nothing on it—except a single golden triangle. She excitedly turned the page and read the book's first sentence:

Agent Maddie, this is an urgent communiqué. Report to Camp Minerva immediately.

Maddie gasped and cheered at the same time, which came out sounding like a loud, awkward cough. Her teacher and classmates stared at her, but she merely smiled and asked, "May I be excused?"

Her next mission had just begun. . . .

ACKNOWLEDGMENTS

Max Mason wishes to thank this super secret super team of people for helping bring Maddie's adventure to life:

The incomparable Karen Chaplin for her super editorial eye, and the amazing group at HarperCollins Children's Books, including editorial director Rosemary Brosnan, designer Joel Tippie, production editor Kathryn Silsand, and all of sales, marketing, and publicity.

The notorious Doug Holgate for his ingenious illustrations.

The masterful Sara Shandler, Josh Bank, Laura Barbiea, Joelle Hobeika, Romy Golan, and Les Morgenstein at Alloy Entertainment.

The magnificent Eliza Swift, Drew Welborn, Chris Hernandez (for loving this story first), Adam Rubin, Temis Galindo, Daniel Kibblesmith, Jennifer Wright, Norman Weiner, Robin Braunstein, and Mollie Weiner.

A special thanks to Melissa Thomson and Rachel Ekstrom for their brilliance.

And finally, to you, the reader. You are special and capable of anything. Don't let anyone tell you otherwise.